OFF-LIMITS TO THE GRIZZLY

OBSESSED MOUNTAIN MATES

ARIANA HAWKES

Imprint: Independently published

ISBN: 9798866129355

Cover art: Thunderface Design

www.arianahawkes.com

Blair

"Come on, Blair. I'm short-staffed. You'd be doing me a big favor." My boss, Adrian's voice comes from just behind my right shoulder.

I go still, halfway through pulling a rack of steaming beer glasses from the washer. A drop of ice shoots down my spine. *Is he really bringing this up again?* "No, not happening," I reply.

"You could just... wear a bra-top or something."

I spin around and give him my coldest stare. "I said, the answer is no." I say it loud, to make sure he hears me this time.

His eyelids do a weird spasm. "No need to get all sassy on me."

I clench my jaw. "No need to try and *manipulate* me." What's gotten into him? He even told me when I interviewed for the job that they have topless Wednesdays, but he hires different staff for that night. Said it was a long-running thing he'd acquired from his predecessor. He made a face like he hated it, but *what could you do?* It's a big crowd-pleaser.

He tilts his head and stares openly at my boobs. "You'll get *awesome* tips."

"I don't care." I fold my arms across them.

His face darkens. "What's the big deal, Blair?"

My mouth falls open. "Seriously? What's the big deal?" I splutter. "Uh, the fact they're mine and I get to choose who sees them."

He shrugs. "Show 'em to one guy, might as well show 'em to everyone."

I goggle at him. "Um, that's not how it works for most women." As it happens, no guy has seen them before. But I'm not about to admit to that. And Adrian is really starting to freak me out. He's different tonight. Up until now, he's been like a big brother. A little nerdy, but kind. He's also been my roommate for the past six weeks. We watch movies together and eat popcorn, for christsakes. I thought we *got* each other. But now, there's a weird light in his eyes. Is he high?

"I'm not getting my tits out for money, and that's final."

"Don't forget, I took you in and gave you a place to stay."

"Uh, you hired me and rented your spare room to me."

He sighs. "Not even to help a guy out?"

"Not even to help a guy out." I make my voice hard, hoping it'll signal that I'm done with this bullshit.

He shakes his head sadly. "You're breaking my heart, Blair."

And just like that, the Adrian I know is back again. The porn-king swagger is gone, and I remember he's that guy I chill with on the couch, laughing hysterically and quoting lines from our favorite movies.

DON'T STARE, *don't stare*, I remind myself the following evening, as I trudge down the stairs that lead from my apartment to the rear of the bar. I've agreed to work the shift, fully clothed. No ifs or buts. I don't feel comfortable with this, at all. But hopefully it's a one-off, and I guess I'll have to start looking for another job tomorrow.

Well, this was not what I was dreaming of when I moved out to Oakdale. I thought living here would be the new start I needed, after I lost basically everyone I cared about. First, my best friend, Kayla, left our little hometown. Then my parents died in a car crash, in a fog of cheap bourbon. Then my grandma died, too.

There was nothing keeping me in Twin Falls, so I decided to be like Kayla. She was always the crazy one, while I was the sensible one, but we were inseparable. When she disappeared, I felt like I lost a part of myself. So, I went out into the world, trying to be as free and impulsive as she was. Now look where that's got me—bullied into working at a titty bar.

I step behind the bar, wearing an extra-loose T-shirt and jeans, just so there's no confusion. And I do a double take. There's the familiar cozy room, all done out in dark wood; the long wooden bartop, with the craft beer taps; the regulars sitting at their usual tables; the small screens showing a bunch of sports. And… there are a bunch of bare tits. At least ten of them. It's such a freaking incongruous sight, I fight back a laugh.

"Uh, hi," I say to the girl standing by the beer taps, pouring a pint of Blue Moon.

"Hey!" She puts down the foaming pint and turns to me with a huge smile. "I'm Peaches." She's tiny, but her tits are huge, like a pair of over-inflated balloons. I can just make out her perky nipples in my peripheral vision. *Don't stare, don't stare.* Focus on the flashing white teeth instead. Nice dental work.

Her pretty forehead furrows and I realize I haven't introduced myself.

"I'm Blair."

Her gaze drops to my T-shirt. "Aren't you gonna, like, get ready?"

"Oh, I am ready. I don't … you know."

"Oh." She nods and gives me a pitying look. "That's too bad."

It is? She turns back to the beer and I look around for customers, for something less controversial to focus my attention on.

After an hour or so, I'm kinda used to it. Guess there's only so many times you can be shocked by the same thing. It's still weird seeing the regulars though, mostly a bunch of decent guys I exchange banter with, watching the half-naked girls like hungry jackals.

I'm just carrying a tray of empty glasses to the bar when Adrian appears from the back.

"Blair—" His voice is loud, slightly slurred.

"Adrian."

"Still wearing your shirt."

My spine stiffens. "As agreed."

He shakes his head. "We didn't agree nothing."

I open my mouth to point out that we very much did, but there's that weird light in his eyes again, and I don't think this is going to end well.

"For the last time, I'm not taking my clothes off," I say, quiet but firm.

A muscle twitches in his jaw and he leans in close. His breath reeks of scotch. "You're a real prick tease, you know that?"

"Errr...what?"

"Blair, you either show 'em the goods, or you get the hell out."

A twizzling red panic alarm goes off in my head. "Uhh, I'll go with option B, then."

Heart sinking, I dump the tray on the counter and head toward the back stairs.

But, quick as a flash, he shoulders his way in front of me.

"Let me get past, Adrian."

"Where d'you think you're going?"

"To my apartment?"

"It's not yours anymore. The room comes with the job."

My gut lurches. Out of a job and homeless at exactly the same moment. Amazing.

Probably for the best, though. I was not looking forward to spending another night under the same roof as my newly psycho ex-boss.

"Okay, I'll just get my stuff then."

"Nope." He plants his hands on his hips, blocking the doorway. "Not happening."

Fuck. I bite down on the end of my tongue. The room is not officially mine. I didn't sign a lease. I was broke. I didn't have a security deposit. Adrian let me move in and said he'd take the rent out of my paycheck.

"Come on, Adrian, be reasonable. I don't even have my coat here."

"Tough titty." He stares at my boobs and leers like he's cracked an amazing joke.

"Hey, Adrian!" one of the topless girls calls.

Scowling in annoyance, he looks for her.

I feel in my pocket for my key. I'll go out through the main door, get into the apartment through the street entrance. Then I can bolt the front door and keep Adrian out while I'm gathering up my stuff.

"Barrel needs changing," she hollers. He takes a step toward her.

I turn and *run.*

I'm there. My hand is curling around the brass doorhandle, a blast of freezing night air is pouring in, and…

A strong arm wraps around my waist. I smell Adrian's breath as he pulls me back inside.

"No, you don't." His voice is low and sinister. Almost

unrecognizable. "Now, quit making a scene and come with me. You have no idea who I really am, Blair."

A whole glacier's worth of ice shoots down my spine. *Crap.* Is he bluffing, or does he mean that? How was I so wrong about him? I thought my psycho radar was pretty good.

Apparently not.

Gooseflesh breaks out all over me as I go limp and allow him to turn me around and walk me back to the bar. My eyes dart everywhere, looking for help.

But no one's paying us any attention, of course. The bar is packed, but the only thing the customers are looking at right now is tits.

"You're gonna go out back, take off your top, and come back out and serve the drinks like a good girl," Adrian snarls in my ear. If he's trying to channel Kilgrave from Jessica Jones, he's doing a damn good job.

Double fuck.

How the hell am I going to get out of this one?

He shoves me behind the bar, and through the narrow passage that leads to the back rooms.

I look out for one of the girls. Maybe I can get them to call the cops for me?

Who am I kidding? There's no way I'm gonna get them in trouble with Psycho Eyes.

"Open the door," he snarls. I fumble the handle on the door that leads to the office. The door swings open and...

There's someone in there. A hulking, massive-shoul-dered guy in a leather jacket. He's just standing there, feet wide apart, hands hanging loose at his sides. In a flash I take in longish salt-and-pepper hair, and a beard that covers the lower half of his face.

Gulp. What the hell is Adrian planning to do with me? I start to shake like crazy.

"Who the fuck are you?" Adrian demands, over my shoulder.

My heartbeat slows. Okay, not something Adrian had planned for me.

But who the heck is this giant?

"Get the hell off her," he growls.

"Get the fuck out of my office!" Adrian retorts. Kinda brave, considering the guy is almost double his size.

The guy takes a step closer, pushes up the sleeves on his jacket. "I didn't want to make a scene out there, upset all those poor girls." He jerks his head toward the bar. "But that's the only reason I'm being so patient with you." He enunciates each word carefully. His voice is low, but threatening, and his face gets extra-hard and feral looking. He's real powerful. Not psycho-scary, what-the-fuck-is-he-gonna-do-next powerful. But he radiates this awesome strength. I get the sense he could pulverize Adrian without even trying. "I won't tell you again. Get your filthy hands off her."

I stare at him in confusion. What does he want with me? Maybe Adrian owes him some money and he's come to take me as payment in kind?

But no, that's not right. There's something familiar about him. Real familiar—

His hand shoots out and grabs Adrian's shoulder.

"Aggh!" Adrian screams, and immediately releases me. There's a crash as his knees hit the floor.

Go! I sprint for the door.

"Blair, go up to the apartment, grab your stuff. My truck's parked right outside."

I freeze, goggling at the guy.

He knows my name.

He looks hella familiar.

Because I know him.

Mr Johnson.

The father of my ex-best friend.

Suddenly my legs don't feel strong enough to hold me up.

I haven't seen him for a long, long time. Not since he yelled at me, and told me to stay away from Kayla. He scared the hell out of me. He's changed a lot. The hair, the beard, the little creases at the corners of his eyes. That's why I didn't recognize him at first. But now I take in those piercing blue eyes, and that hard, uncompromising jaw hiding behind his beard. Of course, it's him. And he's only gotten more handsome over the years.

"Go on, I'm taking you home," he says in a softer voice.

Home?

The big city has chewed me up and spat me out. I don't have a home. Not the small town I was raised in. Not anywhere.

"You're safe now," he continues.

I take a deep breath, give him one final look, and *bolt*.

2

Zachary

I close my eyes for a beat, tune my ears in, and listen to the sound of Blair's feet running up the stairs overhead. Good.

Then I return my attention to the quivering heap of crap at my feet.

"What are we going to do with you?"

His lips are pulled back from his teeth like a cornered animal. "I didn't do anything to her."

"Like hell you didn't."

"I-it wasn't a big deal. All the chicks love working here. All the tips and the attention from the guys."

I work my jaw. I'm a step away from busting out of my skin, but I'm gonna do my best to contain my beast. "But she said no. And you were about to take away her right to decide what she does with her own body."

He narrows his eyes. "You her father or something?"

I take a breath, as memories of Blair crash over me like a thunderstorm. "As good as," I say at last.

He raises his hands. "Look, I overstepped, alright. I won't do it again."

I shrug off my jacket and take a step toward him. "No, you won't."

FIVE MINUTES LATER, I stride through the bar and out into the cold night. Adrian is still in one piece, but he might think twice about abusing his female staff again. My heart is pounding beneath my ribcage, and my beast won't quit pacing and snarling. It was hell getting it to go back inside me just now.

It's all riled up, desperate to lay eyes on Blair again.

She's there. A sigh of relief bursts out of me. Standing beside my truck, a duffle bag laying on the sidewalk beside her. So small and vulnerable looking. And she's shivering. Damn. I click the fob and the door locks clunk open.

She shoots me a wild glance, questions flashing in her eyes. There'll be time for all that later.

I dart toward her, open the door. "Get in, honey."

She hesitates a second longer, then she clambers in.

I go around, jump in the driver's seat and shut the door, and it's just the two of us, alone together in this little space.

Her scent fills my nostrils. That citrus-musk perfume she wears, and the rich, clean smell of her hair.

This is the closest I've been to her since she was still in her teens, and I was starting to have some thoughts about her that were not appropriate at all.

Now she's an adult, glowing with a mature, womanly beauty. Her hair has lost its teenage frizz and hangs in glossy waves the color of maple syrup. She's also quit wearing heavy make-up and her golden-brown eyes are more lovely than ever.

But right now, they are wide and stunned. "W-what just happened?"

I start up the car. It's a long drive home and the sooner we get going, the better.

I turn over my thoughts. This will take some explaining. She doesn't need to know I've been watching over her ever since she left Twin Falls.

"I saw how that asshole was coercing you, and I put a stop to it," I say at last.

"You were drinking in the bar?"

"Yup."

She blinks several times. "I've never seen you there before."

"Oh, I was just passing through. Not my kinda place." I give a dry laugh.

"I-I don't usually work the topless night," she says quietly. "But Adrian talked me into it, and then…" She trails off. I see her chest heave.

"I heard it all, hun, you don't need to explain."

"He got real weird. He's never been like that before."

I crook an eyebrow. "He was probably all Mr Nice Guy before that, huh?"

"Yeah." She injects so much embarrassment and dismay into the word, it breaks my heart.

"It's not your fault, Blair. Some guys are just like that."

"Thank you for saving me, Mr Johnson," she says after a beat.

Mr Johnson.

I stop breathing. "You can call me Zach. We're both adults now."

"Z-Zach. She rolls my name around her mouth. Jesus. That shouldn't feel so good. "Where are you headed?"

"Back to Twin Falls," I say.

"Oh…" Her shoulders slump. "I left there a long time ago."

I know.

"So you're based in Oakdale now?" I ask.

She sighs. "Yeah. But now I don't have a job, or a place to live. I was supposed to be making a new life here, but it's been hard…"

She twists her fingers in her lap, stares out of the side window. "Maybe you could drop me at a motel or something—?"

"I'm taking you back to Twin Falls," I cut her off, and her breath catches. Crap. That was too loud. But no way in hell am I leaving her in a motel here. She's under my protection now.

"I can't. I mean, I don't have a place to stay there. And… I just can't go back. I'll feel like such a failure." Her chest rises and falls rapidly, and I fight the urge to pull over and take her in my arms.

Instead, I clear my throat. "Blair, listen to me. You're not a failure. The girl I knew was strong and kind and loyal, and I'll bet my bottom dollar that hasn't changed. Come back with me for now. We'll put an action plan together, and then you can decide on your next move."

Her eyes flash onto mine, with a flicker of something—hope, I think.

"I've got a spare room for you," I say.

Silence rings out between us.

"You can stay as long as you like," I add.

She shakes her head. "Why are you helping me?"

"Because you need help." That's the truth.

"But, last time I saw you—"

I close my eyes for a beat as the past rushes over me like hot lava. So much shame and confusion. I yelled at her to get out, to stay away from my daughter. The pain and sadness on her face has been seared into my brain for eternity.

"I'm sorry for what happened back then," I mutter. "It was a difficult time."

I hear a hitch in her breathing.

"Have you heard from Kayla since she left?" she says.

"Yeah, from time to time."

"I haven't," she says quietly. "She said I'm better off without her."

Her words twist a knife in my gut. I'm sorry to say it of my own daughter, but I think she was right. I'm so sorry Blair wound up being hurt though.

"You two turned out pretty different," I say at last.

She exhales heavily. "We used to be so close. We

shared everything. But when we got to about thirteen, she changed. She got real wild."

I nod. *Because Kayla is a big cat and she just hit puberty.*

"You lost your parents, didn't you?" I ask, making my voice soft. I heard it on the grapevine right after it happened.

"Yeah. Car crash. They were both drunk." She says it tonelessly, like any emotion has long been wrung out of her.

"I'm so sorry."

She shrugs. "They were never real parents. All they cared about was drinking and getting high."

I knew that. That's why I used to try and give her some stability, let her stay at our place whenever she wanted.

"Then I went to live with my grandma for a few years. But then she died. Selling her trailer didn't even cover her debts. So…" She throws her hands out, helplessly.

"I know things have been rough, but it'll be different now. Twin Falls is a nice place these days. It's gotten real civilized. There's even a yoga studio."

She giggles. "I don't know. So many bad memories there. I wanted a new start…"

"Give it a chance," I say, and my thoughts are already turning over, wondering what I can do to make her so happy in Twin Falls that she never thinks of leaving again.

"Were you planning to drive overnight?" she asks suddenly.

Darn. She was always as bright as a button and my story doesn't exactly hold water.

"There's supposed to be a storm coming," I say at last. Not a lie.

Now my plan is to get her back to Twin Falls as soon as possible. Guess I could book us into a motel for the night, but I can hardly get her to share my room, and there's no way I'm gonna leave her in a room by herself.

She nods, seems to accept that, and shuffles down into her seat like she's making herself more comfortable.

A few minutes later, her breathing slows. A little smile tugs at my lips. She must trust me, at least a little.

It is a long drive back to Twin Falls, the dark road unspooling endlessly between fields crusted in snow, but I enjoy every moment of it. My beast is quiet inside me, for the first time in a long, long time. After years of keeping watch over her, Blair is finally under my protection. And I'm not going to screw it up this time.

3

Blair

 wake up slowly. I feel so relaxed, so peaceful. Well, that's weird. Not a typical feeling these days—or for as long as I can remember, actually. I'm sitting half upright, snuggled under something warm and heavy that smells of leather and spice. Where am I?

Ohh, I know—

At the last moment, I stop myself from jerking upright. Mr Johnson—uh, Zach; although I don't think I'll ever be able to call him that—is right beside me, driving us back to Twin Falls. How long have I been asleep? I open my eyes a crack and peer through my eyelashes. It's still dark, but there's hint of gray in the sky now, and I can make out some red taillights in the distance. A long time, I guess.

There I was, snoozing, while he was driving.

I don't dare turn my head and look at him, but I'm so aware of his huge bulk beside me. When I was a kid, I thought he was the biggest man in the world. Now I'm grown up... pretty much the same.

He's one of those guys who has presence. When he walks into a room, every head turns to look at him. When I was a teen, I was scared of him. There was a lot of tension between him and Kayla, and he suddenly got all strict and shouty. She said he was a real disciplinarian. But the more rules he gave her, the more she rebelled.

He's been so kind to me, though. And so protective. I didn't ask him what he did to Adrian and honestly, I don't want to know. I was just so, so glad when he appeared at the truck, like my knight in shining armor. The moment the door locks clicked into place, I felt *safe*.

Which is weird, because now I feel all kinds of jumpy. Especially when I pick up that scent of his, wafting off the leather jacket he must've thrown over me.

Kinda wish he hadn't gotten even more good looking in the past decade. He used to be clean-shaven, with cropped dark hair, but this salt-and-pepper thing he's got going on is just...

Oof... there goes a little tingle between my thighs. Fuck.

Truth is, I used to have an embarrassing crush on him. When I got to about sixteen, I started noticing that he wasn't just Kayla's dad; he was the most attractive guy I'd ever laid eyes on.

Whenever Kayla wanted to gossip about the boys

she liked, all I could think about was her dad. Once I mentioned that he was handsome and Kayla went crazy. Like, totally freaked out.

Don't you ever think of my dad like that! she screamed.

After that, I got real awkward when I was around him. Every time he spoke to me, my cheeks would go beet red. And I'd try to get away from him as fast as I could.

Hope I don't start to like him again—

Although, something tells me it's already too late.

A ROAD SIGN looms out of the darkness.

Twin Falls.

My stomach fizzes.

I was planning to never see Twin Falls again. But as soon as Mr Johnson said, *I'm taking you home,* in that growly voice of his, I knew I wasn't going to argue.

We pass a familiar mom-and-pop gas station. Then Harding's furniture store. Then Meadows Restaurant.

Home. The word rises in me. It comes from somewhere deep in my chest. And it fills me with all kinds of longing and sadness. I know this place, in a way that I never got to know Oakdale. Guess I'm just a small-town girl, after all.

Mr Johnson turns off the main road, onto a dirt track. That's weird; I don't remember this area. His place is on the other side of town. I keep quiet. Right now, I don't really trust myself to speak, anyway.

We pass into a forest of pine trees. Big old trunks, shooting up to the sky, packing the road on either side.

Mr Johnson takes a bunch of turns, bringing us deeper and deeper into the forest.

At last, he slows and pulls up. We're in front of a cabin. A very familiar cabin.

My eyes fly wide open and I haul myself upright, as I take in the dark wood front door, the little square windows, the tiny porch. This was our den—Mine and Kayla's. We found it one day while we were wandering around the forest. Kayla called it our clubhouse. She was obsessed with it. She used to bring stuff to do it up and make it real cozy, and she made me promise not to tell anyone else about it.

"Welcome back, sleepyhead." There's an undertone of amusement in Mr Johnson's voice.

I sure hope I didn't embarrass myself when I was asleep. Snoring or muttering about how sexy he is or something.

"Sorry," I mumble. "I didn't mean to fall asleep."

"I could tell you needed it."

He sounds so soft, so kind, I startle, and next thing I know, I'm staring right into those piercing eyes of his.

Annd....my cheeks are burning again. *Crap.* Is it going to be like that every time I look at him?

That's gonna get real awkward.

"What are we doing here?" I blurt out.

"Does it look familiar?" he asks, all innocence.

"I-I didn't think you knew about it."

He laughs. "Well, I let you girls think that. I wanted you to have your own space. But, of course, I was keeping an eye on you."

I blink. Kayla was so fearless walking around the

forest, even on those pitch-black evenings in winter, when there was no moon. It was like she was daring the universe to throw something at us. Meanwhile, I thought it was as creepy as hell, and I was only there to keep her company. But all that time her dad was actually watching over us?

Mr Johnson climbs out of the truck and I follow.

The front path used to be nothing but dirt, but now it's paved with little stone tiles. When he pushes open the front door, a rush of warm, sweet-scented air rushes out. Unexpected. I was preparing myself for mildew and rot.

Inside, the old place is transformed. It was real rundown when Kayla and I found it. A lot of the wooden boards were rotten through, and we patched up some of the broken windowpanes with plastic sheeting. But now, it's beautiful. There's a brand-new kitchenette, and it looks like a fire was recently burning in the hearth. There are a bunch of fur rugs on the floor, and the living area has a nice leather couch, armchairs, and a coffee table.

"Wow," I say.

"I did some renovations."

"It's real nice."

He grunts, like he's embarrassed, but pleased.

I wander through the cabin. It's been a while, but I don't remember there being a passageway at the back. "Is this an extension?"

"Yeah. I needed a little more space here."

Without stopping to think, I push open the door at the rear.

It's a bedroom. All done out in wood paneling, with a pretty plaid curtains and a huge, king-size bed, covered in a downy white comforter.

"Ohh—" I spin around, startled.

Mr Johnson is lingering in the main room, elbow propped against the door frame. "I live here full-time now."

"What about the old place?"

He shrugs. "Sold it."

"B-but why? It was such a beautiful house," I say, remembering how much I used to love playing there as a kid. Hanging out in the den with Kayla. Sitting in the huge kitchen-diner, chatting to Mr Johnson and helping him prepare those delicious stews he used to make.

"After my wife, and then Kayla left, it got too big for me, all by myself. Too many ghosts."

He gives a dry laugh, but I catch a shadow of pain chasing across his handsome features.

"It's not a lot, but it's enough for me," he continues.

"And this room?" I point at the other door, the one that's closed.

"Go ahead," he says.

I push it open, step inside, and gasp.

It's full of Kayla's stuff. Her old childhood bedroom has basically been recreated in here—the white filigree bedframe; the pink velvet armchair; the Halestorm and Evanescence posters on the walls; the battered old pinboard. I pick up a sparkly silver photo frame from her old nightstand. Behind the glass is a photo of the two of us. I know it well. We're in Mr Johnson's old yard, and it's a beautiful fall day. The two of us are clutching each other and giggling. Probably at some silly joke that nobody would get, but us. Kayla's hair is brick red. I remember she'd just dyed it, and her green eyes are sparkling with mischief.

All of a sudden, my own eyes tear up. Despite everything, I still miss her so much.

"It probably looks like a shrine or something," Mr Johnson says, rubbing at the back of his head.

"No, it's really, really nice," I say.

"Just couldn't bring myself to throw all her old stuff away." Then he says, so quietly I almost miss it, "guess I hoped she might come back one day."

"Oh, Mr Johnson."

He sits heavily on the bed and I join him. I've got the strongest urge to throw my arms around him.

His shoulders are slumped and he stares down at Kayla's fluffy white area rug. "You must've missed her when she left?"

"Like crazy," I say. "And I felt so guilty."

His head snaps toward me. "But why?"

Automatically I turn mine too, and that lightning-bolt shock hits me again. Energy crackles from his ice-blue gaze, and I don't trust myself to keep looking into his eyes. He's so close I can feel the heat coming off his powerful body.

My heart is pitter-pattering beneath my shirt, making me all jittery.

"Because I should've made her stay," I manage to say.

His forehead crumples. "Oh, sweetie, there was nothing you could do to make her stay. It was Kayla's time to leave."

"What do you mean?"

Emotions pass across his face, too quick for me to identify them. "There are some things I should tell you. But later. I need to go out, get some food. And you probably need to sleep some more."

"Oh, I'm okay. Are you going to the supermarket? I can come with—"

"Stay here," he says, in a voice that brooks no disagreement.

I swallow hard. This is like the Mr Johnson of old.

Only now, my body is responding in a very different way. Somehow, I kinda like the thought of him bossing me around. Telling me what's best for me.

He bounds to his feet in that agile way of his, and strides out of the room. "Sleep in the main bedroom if you want," he calls over his shoulder.

I frown. "But isn't that yours—?"

The front door slams shut.

And I'm alone.

I stare at the photo of Kayla and me for a long, long time.

I've got feelings for your father, I tell her silently. *Very inappropriate feelings.*

And what the hell am I going to do about that?

4

Zachary

I'm gone a long while, because the traffic was heavy, then I was an age in the supermarket, figuring out what Blair might want to eat. When I get back to the cabin, I park up fifty yards away and walk the rest of the way. I don't want to risk waking her up if she's still sleeping.

The moment the little log building comes into view, I feel my beast fighting for dominance. Nostrils snuffling hungrily, claws tearing at the dirt in its impatience to get back. To get to Blair.

I shove it back down, self-disgust pouring through me.

These feelings for Blair aren't wholesome. Aren't right.

She's a kid I'm watching out for.

This is wrong, all the way to hell and back.

Not a kid. A grown woman, my animal reminds me.

I snarl at it. She is a woman, though. However hard I've tried not to look, Blair's ripe curves are any man's dream. That perfect hourglass figure; the flash of cleavage at the neck of her shirt. Those full, pouting lips. She's so lush and tempting. Like a juicy peach, just about to drop off a tree.

Honey-sweet and begging to be touched.

For years, I've been looking out for her from a distance, telling myself that the magnetic pull I felt toward her was platonic. But now I'm up close to her, it's on a whole other level.

It's consuming. It's like nothing else in the world exists, but her. My eyes seek her out constantly. My hands ache to touch her velvety skin. My lips burn to press against hers. This is nothing I've felt before. I want to possess her. Make her a part of me. Need and longing rush through my veins endlessly.

The whole time I was driving to the store, shopping for stuff and coming back again, she was all I could think about. Every moment was full of memories, impressions of her. Her sweet scent, her mischievous laugh. The way she looks at me sometimes, kind of stunned. Damn. I'm obsessed.

But hasn't that been the truth for years? Hasn't she been my number one priority, ever since Kayla left?

I just hadn't expected it to turn into something physical. Sexual.

I walk along the paving stones to the front of the cabin, listening for her. It's all quiet though, and the cabin is dark inside. She must still be sleeping, poor thing, exhausted after last night's drama.

I go around to the back, treading carefully through the deep layer of fall leaves. There's a nip in the air; the first snow of the season will be coming soon. I check the log walls as I go. I've made sure the cabin is well insulated, but now Blair is staying here, I'm gonna make sure it's the coziest log cabin that ever was. She deserves every little bit of comfort she's missed out on in her life so far.

When I approach the window of the main bedroom —my bedroom—I hear the sound of her breathing. But it's quicker than I would've expected. Is she having a nightmare or something?

I take another step and peer through the darkened glass...

And my eyes just about fall out of my head.

Blair is still lying in bed. But the covers are thrown off her body.

She's wearing nothing but her underwear.

And her panties are pushed to one side. Because her hand is between her sweet thighs, moving rhythmically back and forth.

She's touching herself.

Fuck.

A spasm of desire, like nothing I've felt in my life before, shoots through me.

She gasps and jerks upright.

Crap. She must've caught the flicker of movement.

And now we're locking eyes.

I bolt away from the window, guilt spilling through me like lava.

How the hell am I going to explain to her that I wasn't spying on her? That I wasn't being some dirty old pervert?

I trudge around to the front door on heavy legs.

Shit, this is bad. After that sleazebag at her job as well? She's gonna think I'm just like him.

Maybe I don't have to face her right now.

I can just drop off the shopping bags inside the door.

Yeah, that's a good idea.

I open the front door and slide them in.

Just as a light flicks on.

She's standing in the doorway of the bedroom, wearing her jeans and shirt again.

I'm gonna try not to notice that the zipper is undone and I'm getting another glimpse of her lacy panties. Her lips are red and her cheeks are all pink. She's a goddess. A tiny, womanly goddess. And my bear is scrabbling inside me, desperate to get at her. *She's aroused*, it tells me. *Ready.*

No shit? If my rough ol' face hadn't just appeared at the window like an almighty pussy blocker, she'd be in her happy place right now.

Orgasming.

Damn, I'm trying so hard not to think of her sweet young pussy spasming in ecstasy. How it would feel if my cock happened to be buried in it at that exact same moment—

"I'm so sorry, Mr Johnson!" she gasps out.

"Zach—" I break off. I can't exactly remind her to

call me Zach when we're in the middle of discussing her masturbatory habits.

"I promise it won't happen again."

I open my mouth and close it again.

I'd sure be sorry if Blair never touched her little pussy in my bed agai—.

Stop.

I need to quit with these dirty thoughts.

She's the same age as my daughter.

Which means I'm a dirty old pervert.

But—

It doesn't feel like that.

It just feels *right*. This feeling I've never had in my life before is pouring through my veins.

I feel like Blair is the one. The one I'm supposed to be with.

I didn't feel it before, because she was just a kid. But now, now she's a mature woman—

I feel like I can hear the voice of the world in my ear, telling me I'm too old for her and I should know better. But my heart and my beast are telling me she's mine.

I clear my throat, but my voice still comes out hoarse. "I'm the one who needs to apologize. I'm very sorry I intruded on you, Blair. I was checking whether you were still asleep, because I didn't want to disturb you."

"Oh—" She drops her gaze to the floor. "I slept for a couple of hours. Then, I-I don't know what came over me."

"It's perfectly natural," I say. Then I remember when Kayla was getting to puberty—how I read a book called

Educating your teen about sex. You were supposed to tell them that exploring their own body was a healthy part of growing up.

A lot of good it did. The first time I broached the topic, she completely freaked out and made me promise never to mention it again.

Who would've thought that all these years later, I'd be passing on that same advice to her best friend?

"What's funny?" Blair demands. Damn. She thinks I'm laughing at her, and she looks like she's about to cry. The poor girl is probably totally humiliated.

I wish I could tell her that this has been the sexiest, most arousing moment of my whole life. And if she wanted to take me back to the bedroom while she finished herself off, I'd be in there like a shot.

Instead, I mumble, "Nothing," and I turn my back on her and get busy putting all the groceries away. There's a bunch of moldy stuff at the back of the fridge. I pull it out and shove it into a garbage bag. I've barely been here since Blair left town. I've either been sleeping in my truck or in a motel somewhere close to her place, keeping watch over her.

When I get back from dumping the garbage outside, she's nowhere to be seen, but I can hear the shower going.

Darn. The thought of her naked in the shower is more than my bear can stand right now.

And a bad, bad thought bursts into my mind—will she finish off in there? Is she gonna grace my little shower cubicle with her orgasm? I sure hope so.

I get to work in the kitchen, prepping a bunch of

vegetables. She hasn't been eating well lately, my girl. She's been mainly living on takeout and the food from the bar where she worked. It's okay I guess, but no substitute for a home-cooked meal.

I'm going to cook her something real tasty tonight. When she was a kid, she used to love strong flavors. Unlike Kayla, who was a burger and pizza addict, Blair always wanted to try new things.

She's gone a long time. To my beast's disappointment, I don't hear any little sighs or moans, but when she finally reappears, her eyes are still downcast.

"You look all brand-new," I tell her. It's true; she must've taken off her make-up or something, and she looks all fresh, like a chick that just came out of the egg.

But I'm mostly saying it in the hope it'll draw a line under what happened before.

"Want a beer?"

"Yes," she says, fast.

I reach into the fridge, grab an IPA and pop off the cap with my teeth.

"Oh, that's my favorite," she says.

I know. There's little craft beer shop in Oakdale. She used to go in there sometimes and browse the shelves. Every time the clerk checked out her ass, it was all I could do not to tear his head off. She'd spend a long time deciding, but she'd always wind up choosing the same beer. And she only ever bought one, like it was a special treat for herself. Used to warm my heart to think of her going back home and savoring it.

"Happens to be my favorite, too." Of course, I made

sure to try it as well, and it was delicious. She's got good taste, my girl.

But I shouldn't call her that.

"Can I help?" she says.

"Only by keeping me company," I say, and I direct her to a seat at the kitchen table.

I can't wait for the food to be ready so I can sit down opposite her, and we can talk.

At last, the Thai red curry is done to perfection.

She's set the table. She's even found an old candle and shoved it in a holder I didn't know existed.

"We used to light candles a lot," she says with a smile. "We thought we were being real discreet, keeping the lights down low."

I stay silent, remembering those nights, where I'd check in periodically, making sure I could see two small female silhouettes lit from behind the curtains, and no more.

Blair starts eating ravenously. "Wow, this is so good. The best thing I've eaten since... since..." She frowns, staring into space. "Since you last cooked for me," she says, and we both laugh. She's adorable.

"I can cook for you every day from now on," I tell her.

She looks startled. Was that too much? Am I giving away just how fixated I am on her?

"Or you can cook if you want," I continue.

She grins. "I sure miss cooking. The kitchen in my last place wasn't very well stocked. And I don't know... I just didn't feel comfortable cooking there."

Something flashes in her eyes.

"You're perfectly safe here, Blair," I say. "This place is reinforced. I made sure of that. It could keep out a whole pack of bears."

Reflexively, she gazes out of the darkened window and I see a shiver going through her.

"So isolated out here," she murmurs, wrapping her arms around herself.

"Doesn't it feel like home?"

"Yeah," she says slowly. "It feels different now. When I was here with Kayla I always felt like she was going to lead me into danger—" She breaks off, her cheeks reddening. "Oh, I'm sorry, I didn't mean to imply anything bad about her."

"It's okay," I tell her. "I understand, believe me. It was in Kayla's nature to seek out danger." I work my jaw back and forth. Now is the moment to tell her the truth about Kayla's true nature. But that will mean telling her about me, too, and I can't stand to see her beautiful eyes cloud with horror and disgust.

"Saw a couple of places in town that are hiring," I say instead.

Confusion sweeps her face. "Oh, I... I'm not sure if I'm staying here long."

My bear howls inside me.

"You probably need some time to get used to things," I manage to say calmly.

"I guess you're right." She gives me a thin smile. "There are just so many sad memories here."

We could make some new memories, I want to tell her. *Build something beautiful together.*

Suddenly, there's so much guilt in her eyes it knocks me sideways.

"What is it, sweetie?" I demand.

"Did Kayla leave because of me?"

"What—of course not," I start to say.

Then she bursts into tears.

I don't stop to think. I dart over to her. Crash down on the floor on my knees and pull her tiny body into my arms.

And she clings to me.

She holds me tight, like she's drowning and I'm a life raft.

The feel of her is incredible. So soft and petite and curvy. Her hair is like silk, and I can feel her eyelashes fluttering on my neck.

Hell, if this girl wants to use me as a life raft, I'm all in.

"It's okay, honey." I whisper reassuring words into her ear, rubbing her back in circles, easing her pain away.

Little by little, her sobbing eases.

"Oh, god, I'm so sorry." She draws back and wipes at her eyes with the back of her hand. "After all you've done for me."

"That's the least I'd do for you," I say. That's way too much to tell her, but I don't care anymore.

Now Blair has been in my arms, I know, more than ever that she's the one. There's never been any other. I've been looking for her all my life, and heaven knows I've made some mistakes along the way. But this is right.

This is the real thing. My bear swells beneath my skin, burning to claim her.

Confusion flickers in her golden irises. Questions hang on her beautiful lips.

I don't want to scare her off.

"Mr Johnson?"

My breath shudders in my chest. There's something so darn sexy and wrong about her calling me Mr Johnson all the time. "Uh huh?"

"You're, like, shaking. Are you cold?"

I choke back a purr. She can feel my muscles trembling, feel the effort it's costing me not to drag her mouth to mine and plunge my tongue in deep. Not to tear off her clothes and explore her sweet body for the first time.

I take a deep breath. This is not the time for subterfuge. "No, I'm not cold, Blair."

5

Blair

I stare at the wooden front door for a long, long time. I guess I upset Mr Johnson. Seemed like he couldn't get away from me fast enough.

He looked like he was about to tell me something— something important. But then he sprung to his feet in that quick way of his, and said he was gonna get some rest, and he'd see me in the morning.

But he lives here? Unless I'm real confused, this is his home now.

I didn't even get a chance to ask him where he was planning to sleep, before he stormed out into the dark night.

Was it something I said? I replay our conversation, trying to remember.

He was like that when I was a teen, too. He'd be real

kind, but then he'd suddenly get all hostile and want me out of his sight. It was so confusing.

What a crazy intense evening. My pulse is still fast and jumpy. Being around him makes me so nervous, I was almost glad when he left. But now he's gone, all I can think about is how much I want to see him again.

The feeling of his arms around me.... butterflies fluttered in my stomach and my skin tingled all over.

When I was little, he used to carry me on his massive shoulders and I felt so safe with him.

But now... his touch is exciting.

Dangerous.

Because it makes me want all kinds of things I shouldn't.

When he caught me touching myself, I was so embarrassed, I thought I was gonna die. How would I ever be able to face him again?

But he was actually pretty cool with it.

It's perfectly natural to explore your body. I think of him saying these words in his deep, dark, rumbling voice.

Good thing he didn't know I was fantasizing about *him* exploring my body.

Take all your clothes off and spread your legs for me, Blair.

Fuck. And there goes my clit, tingling like crazy again. I slide my hand into my jeans. Maybe I should finish what I started—

Nope.

Not about to get caught for a second time.

How long was Mr Johnson out there watching me?

Was he spying on me deliberately?

No, that's crazy.

A crazy, crazy fantasy.

I get up and add another log to the fire he made, then I start washing the dishes, hoping to distract myself from these filthy thoughts.

* * *

WHEN I WAKE up next morning, white light is showing between the plaid curtains covering Mr Johnson's bedroom window. I have the sense that something disturbed me, but when I strain my ears, all I can hear are the sounds of the forest.

It took me a long time to fall asleep last night. I felt so bad that I was in Mr Johnson's bed while he was... wherever he was. I wanted to message him and tell him that I'd sleep in Kayla's room, and he should sleep in his own bed, but I realized I don't have his number.

The smell of him between the sheets was also real distracting. Every time I started to drift off, another burst of arousal would hit me again.

So, I wound up touching myself.

Even though I'd promised myself I wouldn't. It was the only way I was gonna get to sleep. I imagined giving Mr Johnson a show, while he watched me through the window. Writhing around, running my hands all over my body. Letting him see everything. Then, when I'd gotten him all wound up, he'd burst through the door and take me savagely. Force his big cock inside me. I bet he's got a humungous cock. He's too all-round massive not to.

My cheeks burn at the memory. I should not be thinking about him like that. There's probably a special place in hell reserved for people who jerk off thinking about their best friend's dad.

I open the curtains a chink.

Holy crap. Mr Johnson is the very first thing I see. And not only that. He's stripped to the waist, and he's chopping wood. Swinging a big old axe over his head, before bringing it down on the block and annihilating each chunk of wood. I stare at him mesmerized. His muscles are huge. Rippling. Shoulders, biceps, abs, all totally stacked. No dad bod in sight. His skin is tan, even though it's winter.

He pauses, wipes his forehead with the back of his hand, and turns his head toward me.

Fuck. I'm still staring. I jerk back, but it's too late. He's seen me.

I lift a hand and give a limp wave.

He waves back.

Then he strides toward the cabin.

I leap out of bed, drag some clothes on, and burst out of the bedroom door.

I'm expecting him to be standing in the kitchen, but he's not there. I yank open the front door, and there he is, in the doorway, one hand braced up against the door frame.

Still shirtless.

Oh, god, I think I'm salivating.

For a moment, his face looks kind of soft, open, but it shuts down again fast.

"Sorry, I—" I try to smooth down my hair. "I probably look like a real mess."

He frowns. "Not at all. You look as fresh as a daisy."

A blast of cold air blows through the door, and I shiver.

His face fills with concern. "I'm sorry, look at me making you all cold."

I dart a glance at his bare torso. Mr Johnson on the other hand, doesn't seem to be cold at all. In fact, I can feel the heat radiating off of him.

"Oh—" He looks down at himself, grabs the shirt that's tied around his waist. Chuckles like it's nothing.

"Guess I don't feel the cold a lot." He wipes his forearm across his damp forehead. "Supposed to be a storm blowing in later, but before that, I was wondering if you wanted to go out and have breakfast in town?"

I bite my lip. "In Twin Falls?" The thought of going back brings an instant knot to my gut. But the way he's looking at me, all kind and good natured, I just melt. "Can you wait ten minutes while I get ready?"

He cocks his head. "Take all the time you like."

"Okay, but please come in—to your own home," I say awkwardly, since he looks like he's planning on staying outside.

He throws out his arms carelessly, like he doesn't care one way or the other, and strides in. As he walks over to the kitchenette, his huge bulk instantly dominates the cabin.

Too much. Being in this little space with him so close that I inhale his sexy masculine scent with every breath is way too much, I think as I bolt for the bathroom.

IT IS KIND of a relief being outdoors. The sky is low and slate gray, and the tang in the air can only mean snow is coming, but at least I can focus on things apart from my totally embarrassing attraction toward Mr Johnson.

We drive through the forest, among dense pines and bare deciduous trees. I used to know these woods like the backs of my hands, I think. Every clearing, every trail.

"Been a long time, huh?" Mr Johnson says, as if he read my mind.

"Yeah. Crazy how Kayla and I hung out here so much."

"She was a creature of the forest," he says. "And I was just relieved she wasn't trying to drag you off to bars."

I go still. *He was protective of me, rather than his daughter?* I feel like I'm just starting to grasp something, but it's still out of reach.

We exit onto a familiar backroad. As we approach Twin Falls, my stomach flips. Last time I was here, I hoped I was seeing the town for the last time.

But now I'm not alone, I remind myself. Mr Johnson is here with me.

He parks up in a lot at the end of Main Street.

"Place I have in mind is just a minute away," he says, scanning my winter coat with a worried look. He's still just wearing a plaid shirt and jeans, and I think it's real sweet that he cares about me being cold.

"I'm tougher than I look," I tell him.

A smile tugs at his lips. "Oh, I know you're tough all right, Blair."

How am I tough? I wonder as I follow his broad back out of the lot. He just witnessed me totally failing at life in the big city, and needing to get rescued by my old friend's dad.

Twin Falls looks prettier than I remembered. It's like a delegation of hipsters moved in and gave it a facelift.

Mr Johnson points out a bunch of places.

"Poppy's Little Coffee House. Think it might be hiring… that clothes store, too. And I know the book-shop used to have a sign up at the window."

My heart gives a little jump. He's trying to help me find a job.

But I'm not planning on staying here.

I'm not gonna mention that though. I'm just going to enjoy this moment of walking down Main Street in Mr Johnson's company. Feeling happier and safer than I've felt in a long, long time.

Well, safe from the outside world anyway.

Safe with Mr Johnson? That's another question. Every minute I spend with him, I feel like I'm getting in deeper and deeper. And it can only end in tears.

He pushes open the door of a cozy-looking diner. I go to catch it from him.

"Ladies first," he says, holding it open for me. I get another funny little jump in my chest. Is that how he sees me now—as a lady?

"Isn't this Deb's Place?" I look around at the stylish vintage décor, remembering a grimy café that reeked of old frying oil.

"Used to be. It's the Palace Diner now," he says happily. "A young couple bought it a couple of years ago and restored it to how it was originally."

He grabs the server and requests the table closest to the window. It's got a reserved sign, but after a short conversation, it's ours.

"This is going to be my treat," I tell him while we scan the menus. I'm desperate to do *something* to thank him for all he's done for me.

"Nuh-uh." He fixes me with a serious expression. "I've known you since you were this high, Blair. No way are you paying."

"What's that got to do with anything?" I mumble, cheeks warming. There I was trying to show him I'm all grown up, and he's making me feel like a little kid again. Probably for the best though. The sooner I can get this dumb crush out of my mind, the better.

There's so much on the menu, I can't decide.

"If I recall rightly, blueberry pancakes used to be your favorite," Mr Johnson says, with a twinkle in his eye.

"Still are." I can't stop the grin from spreading across my face.

"With extra maple syrup?"

"You bet."

And a strawberry milkshake?"

I let out a snort. "I drink coffee these days."

He gives me a long look, kinda wistful. Kinda something else that makes my heart beat faster.

The food comes fast, and it's *so* good.

"Not so bad being in Twin Falls, is it?" he asks.

"Everything feels different here. So much lighter than it used to," I say, as I swallow another forkful of my pancakes.

Mr Johnson's face falls a little bit, then his expression turns all intense. "I can't help thinking Kayla had a lot to do with that."

I puff out my cheeks. "It felt different here when I was with Kayla. Like something bad was always about to happen."

"There's a lot you don't know about her."

"Like what?"

He gives me a long, searching look. "She never told you, did she?" Then he takes breath so deep, it feels painful. It's like he's drawing up his soul from a dark, dark place. When he starts to talk, his voice is ragged.

"We made her promise not to tell another soul, but with Kayla, you never know… she's a big cat shifter. A jaguar."

I literally feel my eyes bulge in their sockets. "A shifter… what?"

He sighs. "I know this is real freaky to hear. But I was thinking maybe you'd heard of shifters because there are so many in this town."

"I mean, I have. But…" I stare off into space. "I'm sure I would've known if my best friend was half jaguar." It sounds so crazy, I laugh.

He cracks his knuckles. "I'm glad she kept her promise. Although it would've made things a little easier now if she hadn't."

"We were so close when we were kids," I murmur, the shock of betrayal burning white hot in my chest.

"My guess is if she didn't tell you, it was to protect you. When she was little, I wasn't sure how she was going to turn out, but when she got to around eleven, I could see she was a lot like her mom. Crazy, wild."

"Sometimes she was so kind. So affectionate," I mutter. "Other times, she was all claws."

He nods sagely. "And when she hit puberty, she was totally out of control. As you know, her mom left when she was a baby, and I had no idea how to raise a little wildcat. She started to have these uncontrolled shifts. Tore the place up—"

"The claw marks in the cabin," I cut in.

"Yup."

"She told me she'd hand carved them."

He gives a wry smile. "That was the main reason why I let her have her privacy in the cabin. God knows I love my daughter. I'd do anything for her, but she's untamable, just like her mom."

"You… you weren't with her mom for long?" I ask, and a weird, jealous feeling rises up in me.

Sadness washes over him. "I was young and dumb. I shouldn't have done it. She wasn't my mate. I should've waited for my mate."

"Who?"

He gives me a long look. "The one I was supposed to be with."

As his piercing eyes burn into mine, the thought hits me like a semi-truck. "You're a shifter, too?"

"Full-blood grizzly."

I close my eyes. Of course. Everything about him says bear. His big powerful body, his deep, rumbling voice. I feel like I already knew, deep down.

"Wait, Kayla is half jaguar and half bear?"

He shakes his head. "She's not my biological daughter, but she doesn't know that. I raised her as my own."

I'm quiet while I process everything. Kayla abandoned by her mom, then Mr Johnson taking care of his ex's unmanageable kid all those years.

"Do you know where Kayla went?" I say at last.

"Probably to find her own kind. Maybe she tracked down her mother. She sends me a postcard from time to time, lets me know she's okay."

I shake my head. "What does she say?"

He gives a dry laugh. "Nothing at all. Just her pawprint—dunked in ink and pressed on the paper."

"Sounds like Kayla."

"Yup."

We both fall silent again.

"A lot to take in," he says after a while. "And…" I follow his gaze to the window. Snowflakes are falling out of the pale sky. Slowly now, but I've lived here long enough to know this is just the beginning.

"We'd better get back to the cabin," he says.

6

Blair

The snow is falling fast by the time we pull up in front of the cabin. Mr Johnson lights the fire right away, then he brings a bunch of logs inside and stacks them up by the front door. "Might be a real blizzard," he says. "Don't want you to have to dig your way outside to get wood."

He straightens up and dusts off his hands. "There's a ton of food in the fridge. You should be nice and cozy in here. You need anything, just holler." He grabs a pad of sticky notes from the side table by the door and scribbles his number down.

My stomach drops.

"You're not going?" I blurt out, as a wave of loss washes over me.

"Yeah." He shrugs. "I'd better get out of your hair."

I frown. "But this is your place and I want you to stay."

"I don't think it's a good idea."

"Why are you like this?" My voice is loud and a little shrill. There are so many emotions charging through me right now, I hardly feel in control of myself.

He goes still. "Like what?"

"Hot and cold. You were the same when I was a kid. You used to be so kind, then suddenly you hated me—" *Oh, god.* I'm close to tears. I break off until the burn behind my eyes passes.

His face kind of crumples. "I never hated you, Blair. Not at all. I pushed you away to protect you."

"From what?"

"I was scared my daughter would be a bad influence on you. And you were turning into a woman…" he trails off.

What does he mean by that?

I swallow, trying to process everything. "And now?"

"Now?"

"Why are you pushing me away?"

I see his Adam's apple bob up and down, but he shoves his hands in his pockets and doesn't answer.

"I don't want to be here alone," I say.

At last, he lets out a huge sigh. "It's not a good idea for me to stay here with you."

"Why not? Just tell me, please!" I cringe at the wail of desperation in my voice.

He sighs. "Because I've got feelings. Inappropriate feelings."

"Toward me?" I whisper because I don't dare say the words aloud.

He nods.

Oh god.

I'm dead.

Mr Johnson is telling me he has feelings for me? My heart is beating so fast I feel like it might explode. "And?"

"And what?" Confusion flashes in his irises. And suddenly, I see that he's quaking. The most powerful man I've ever known is trembling in front of me. *Because of how strongly he feels about me?*

Gooseflesh breaks out all over my arms. Like I'm in a dream, I take a step closer to him, and another.

I'm scared as hell, but I'm not gonna stop now. With trembling fingers, I pop open the buttons on my shirt, so my bra is showing. "What if I feel the same?" I murmur.

"Oh, Blair," he groans, leaning in. "You're destroying me."

And suddenly his mouth is on mine.

Mr Johnson is kissing me.

He's really kissing me.

I've been fantasizing about this moment since I was like thirteen, and nothing that my adolescent brain dreamed up came close to this.

His lips sear mine. Hungry, insistent, snatching my breath away. He holds me tight against his body and plunges his tongue into my mouth, like he wants to draw out my soul. I swear I feel every drop of his need.

Then one of his hands comes up and grasps my

breast. *Oh, god.* The feeling of his thumb chafing at my nipple. He's being rough, but I love it. Love to feel the passion that has lain inside him all this time.

Impatiently, he tugs my shirt off my shoulders, then yanks my entire bra down. My tits spring out, exposed to his gaze. I close my eyes for a beat, so glad he's the first man to ever see them. When his callused fingers touch my bare nipples for the first time, I bite back a moan.

His mouth moves onto my neck and he peppers burning kisses all over my skin, while muttering my name over and over,

Blair, baby.

So beautiful, sweetheart.

Then he crashes down to his knees and his hot mouth latches onto my hard, aching nipple.

I feel like he's devouring me alive, and I freaking love it. I want him to possess every bit of me. Enter me, fill me. I want him so bad it hurts. At the same time, I'm shy to touch him. He's still big, scary Mr Johnson.

When I slide my trembling fingers into his hair, something seems to snap in him. He lets out a ragged groan and reaches for the top button of my jeans.

Fuck.

My pussy is aching so much, it's unreal. I'm so nervous, but I *want* this to happen, like I've never wanted anything before.

Mr Johnson presses kisses all along my bare stomach, his soft stubble tickling my skin. He yanks down the zipper, and pulls the waistband down to my thighs...

And stops.

He lifts his head and looks me in the eyes.

I look down at him dizzily. I can see my bare tits, my pink lacy panties, and Mr Johnson on his knees, eyes burning with wild desire. A sight to knock a girl unconscious.

"You're a virgin," he says, his voice hoarse with need.

"Yeah." A smile pulls at my lips. All these years I've felt like a loser for keeping my V-card. For not popping my cherry at a party like everyone else. But now I'm so glad I've kept it, so Mr Johnson can be my first.

But a look of dismay crosses his face. He shoots up to his feet and takes a big step away from me.

I see it. His… thing. His cock. Stretching out the front of his pants. It's gigantic.

"I shouldn't have done that," he mumbles, stumbling backward.

"I-it's okay. I wanted it."

"It's not okay." He presses a hand across his mouth. "What am I doing? Shit, Blair, put your clothes on." He grabs at my bra and shirt, tries to drag them over my tits.

"I can manage," I bat his hands away, ice darting through my veins.

"I-I'm sorry. I've gotta get out of here." In a flash, he darts away from me, yanks the front door open, and he's gone.

Out into the howling blizzard.

For a long moment, I stand there, stunned, hands over my tits. Then I drag my jeans up my thighs and untangle my bra and shirt. What just happened? It was all fine, until he found out I was a virgin?

Why was that a bad thing?

I feel embarrassed. Kind of ashamed, like I pushed him into this or something. But that's not how it was?

I'm so confused.

And what is he doing, out in the blizzard? I run to the window, push the curtain aside. The snow is falling fast now, driven by the wind. There's no way he could drive in weather like this.

But what's that on the ground? Something dark blue. Is it...?

I open the front door. Right away, a gust of wind tears it out of my grasp. I shiver violently as the chill goes right through my clothes. But I keep going.

Mr Johnson's clothes. His shirt and jeans and boots and socks are lying in a heap on the pathway. "What the...?" I mutter.

Then my brain catches up.

Far in the distance, between the trees, is a big, dark brown shape. And in front of the clothes, a set of huge animal footprints marks the fresh snow. Bear footprints.

Mr Johnson shapeshifted into his bear form—because he was so freaked out by my virginity?

Another gust of wind almost knocks me off my feet. I gather up his stuff and dash back into the cabin.

* * *

I HIDE out in Kayla's room, sitting cross-legged on her bed, cuddling her old Jack Skellington doll, and trying to process everything that's happened. My best friend left because she was a shifter, not because I wasn't enough for her. I realize now, that's what I've believed all these years: that my friendship wasn't enough to make her stay.

And Mr Johnson used to be hostile toward me because he wanted to protect me.

But also because he was attracted to me.

I recall all those moments when I was at Kayla's place and he wouldn't even look at me.

He wants me and he hates himself for it.

I'm not a kid anymore, though. I'm a grown woman. Who's still all wet from his kisses, his touch.

I just wish there was some way I could convince him that what's happening between us is not wrong.

IT'S PAST EIGHT, and he's still not back. Maybe he's never coming back.

The thought of not seeing Mr Johnson again is like a knife in my chest. What will I do if he just, never returns? Wait out the blizzard, then go looking for him on foot? Figure out that he doesn't want to see me again, and drag myself off someplace else?

My stomach starts to grumble, so I rummage in the fridge. It's crammed full of delicious-looking food. I cook up some chicken and vegetables and make a pasta sauce. It takes a while but I've got nothing else to do, apart from wonder whether Mr Johnson has found some shelter from the blizzard, and nurse my aching heart.

When I've finished eating, I add some more logs to the fire. I keep peeking through the window. The sky is slate gray and a blanket of snow covers the pathway and the trees and Mr Johnson's truck. Can bears survive out in a storm like this? Don't they usually hibernate during the winter? I press my nose to the frosty window and a shudder goes through me at the thought of him stuck somewhere, stranded.

"Please come back to me," I whisper.

Worried and antsy though I am, my eyelids get heavy. There's no way I'm sleeping in Mr Johnson's bed though. Instead, I find a woolen blanket in a closet and bring it out to the couch. As I listen to the sound of the gale hammering at the windows, I think I've never felt so alone.

7

Zachary

J’ve fallen for Blair worse than ever before. All these years, she's been the first thing I think about in the morning, and the last thing before I go to sleep. And now I've kissed her, tasted her sweet rosebud nipples, my obsession is on another level.

I'm lost.

Destroyed.

I should never have brought her back to Twin Falls. I should've just stayed in the shadows, looking out for her, quietly taking out anyone who might mean her harm, and letting her live her life in peace.

Stupid. Stupid, stupid. I curse myself with every step I take through this thick, endless snow.

I knew how I felt about her, goddammit. I knew what a hell it was trying to keep my beast under control.

But I just couldn't help myself. I needed to speak to her, communicate with her. Keep her safe.

I promised myself I'd never lay a finger on her, and now I've screwed everything up.

The hurt and confusion on her face when I pushed her away just about cut me in two.

How is she gonna feel now, knowing that I'm a big old pervert?

Not a pervert. Mate, my bear interjects.

Not mate, I tell it. She's too young for me. Still untouched for chrissakes.

The smell of her sweet virgin scent radiating from her pussy was what brought me back to my senses. Made me realize that my dick wasn't gonna be the one to break through her virginity. I don't have that right.

No matter how every nerve in my body tells me she's the one for me.

I made a mistake twenty-six years ago with Kayla's mom. I was young and dumb and dazzled by her wildness. My beast was telling me *no*, but I didn't listen.

Then all those years, I lived alone, celibate. Thinking there was never going to be another for me. I'd gone against my fate, and I'd missed my opportunity.

I was okay with that. Some shifters never find their fated mate, for one reason or another. Some go mad; others live out their lives alone. But I decided I was gonna look out for Blair. That would be enough for me. To see her happy and safe would be my happiness.

But what I hadn't figured was how antsy my beast would get every time some guy cracked on to her. How it would swell with murderous rage.

How am I gonna keep watch over her now—now I know she wants me, too?

It's the darkest part of the night, and the blizzard is only getting worse. Heavy, driving snow, stinging my eyes and muzzle. But my beast plows on, its massive claws churning up the fresh powder. It's tired. It's desperate to find a hollow and sleep for a while.

But I won't quit. I need to keep going. To break whatever's inside of me. This mad passion for a girl I've known all her life.

And if I break myself in the meantime, so be it.

Blair

I WAKE up the next morning, stiff and freezing cold. The blanket slid off during the night and the ashes are cold in the grate. And the blizzard is still going. I lie there listening to it swirling around. Then I run to the window. Wondering... wondering what? Whether Mr Johnson came back last night, and is now huddled on the porch, freezing his ass off?

Hopefully he's indoors somewhere. Staying with a friend or something. Surely he couldn't have stayed out all night in this? The thought sends a shudder through me.

I don't feel like doing anything, but eventually I get myself up. I cook and eat, and I mope around Kayla's room. From time to time, I go lie on Mr Johnson's bed. Wallowing on the soft comforter, imagining what might have been. Imagining if he hadn't freaked out that I was a virgin.

Mid-afternoon, when the light is already failing, I decide to take a bath. I haven't had access to a bathtub for a long, long time, and the one here is huge.

I fill it up, add a squirt of bubbles from the pretty smelling bottle on the side, and climb in.

I float on my back, listening to the howls and whistles of the wind, and the creaks of the cabin as it stands up to the storm.

There's something else. A rap-rap-rapping sound. Like a branch tapping against a window.

I jerk upright, sloshing a ton of water over the side of the tub. Or... like someone knocking on the door.

I jump out, grab my towel and run.

My heart is pounding as I hit the front door.

I don't stop to think. I slide back the latch and yank the door open, and...

A huge, brown beast fills the doorway.

Before I can stop myself, I let out a scream.

It's a bear. A grizzly bear. And it looks exhausted. Its massive body is kind of drooping, its eyes are red-rimmed and heavy, and its muzzle is all crusted with ice.

"Mr Johnson?" I whisper, feeling stupid. For all I know, it might be a regular old grizzly that I'm letting into the cabin to run amok and eat me alive.

It bows its massive head, in what looks like a nod. I exclaim in relief and I open the door wider to let it in.

But something's happening. The bones in its skull are moving, and it's lifting up onto two legs.

Then everything happens in a flash—fur retreating, bones and tendons snapping, a big jerk—and Mr Johnson is standing in the doorway, covered in snow and buck naked.

"Blair—?" he says in a hoarse voice.

"Come in already." I grab his arm, drag him inside and push the door shut behind him. He's probably three times my weight, but he comes with me, like the cold has knocked him senseless.

He stands in the entranceway, feet planted apart. I'm not gonna look down and gawk at that firehose hanging between his thighs. But I can see that he's trembling all over, like some battle-wounded beast. Tenderness pours through me.

He looks tortured, desperate.

Because of me?

The thought hurts my heart.

"I was so worried about you, Mr Johnson!" I exclaim.

"Blair. I'm sorry. I shouldn't have—"

He throws out his hands, then he looks down at himself dazedly, like he's realizing for the first time that, of course, he's naked. "Crap," he growls.

"You're perfect as you are, Mr Johnson," I blurt out.

"I shouldn't let you see me like—"

I let the towel drop.

I didn't plan it like this, it just… happened.

A ragged groan bursts from his lips.

I plant my hands on my hips. I'm shaking like a leaf. No man has seen me naked before, and I'm real glad that Mr Johnson is the first. Even if he freaks out and kicks me out of the cabin, I won't regret doing this.

"Blair, you can't—" His voice is growly with anguish. Deep and rough, and it vibrates right through me, hardening my nipples.

And his cock—I'm still not looking, but in my peripheral vision, I can see it growing, lifting up.

Because it wants to get to me. To go inside me. *Fuck.*

My pussy is aching like crazy and I'm dizzy with how much I want Mr Johnson.

"Too late," I say.

He gives his head a little shake. "You're a goddess. So, so beautiful."

"Just kiss me," I tell him.

A sound rushes from his chest, like a sigh of surrender. He takes a step toward me, holds my head in his hands and presses his lips against mine.

He's gentler this time. He draws my lower lip between his teeth and nibbles on it. Then his tongue flickers softly between my lips. Oh, god. I feel like my soul is lifting up, connecting with his. I angle my head, welcoming him in, wanting him to possess my mouth. Thinking how much I want him to possess my body.

His big rough hands stroke my hair, then move down to my shoulders. "Blair," he mutters. "So goddamn beautiful." He strokes my back and upper arms. I want him to squeeze my tits so much, I'm about ready to beg. But he keeps away from all the parts of me that are burning for his touch.

"Mr Johnson, you can touch me," I say. "I mean, I want you to."

He lets off another of his sexy anguished groans. Then he draws back and looks me in the eye. "You have no idea how much I want to, Blair. None."

Damn, that's sexy. His words run through me like liquid fire. My gaze drops to his cock. It's gigantic. All swollen and pointing up. The slit in the end of it is glistening with moisture. I have no idea how it's going to fit inside me, but I'm ready to find out.

"I want you to be my first," I tell him.

"I can't. I shouldn't even be kissing you." His breathing is ragged as his fingertips drift down to my bare stomach. "Such a sexy little belly, though."

I hold still, willing him to go lower and lower. His fingers drift down, but they come to a stop an inch above the little triangle of hair that I keep neatly trimmed.

"There's a pain between my legs," I say.

He frowns. "What kind of pain?"

"An empty kind of feeling," I say.

"What are you trying to do to me?" he mutters.

I grab his hand and press it between my thighs.

We both give a cry. Me at how good his hand feels on my bare pussy, and Mr Johnson... well, I guess he just discovered how wet I am.

"You want this, huh?" he mutters in a tone of wonder, running his fingertips all over my pussy. I shudder. His touch is ten times better than my own. Before long, I can feel that delicious gathering sensation. I tilt my hips forward, and his fingertip slides into me.

"Holy hell," he exclaims.

His finger feels so good, slipping in and out. Is this how his cock is gonna feel?

"I need you inside me, Mr Johnson," I say, and my voice sounds all thick with need.

The tip of his cock has been pressing against my stomach, but now he jerks away like he's been burned.

"Blair, when bears like me mate, it's supposed to be for life. We don't have one-off sex."

I go still, disappointment hurtling through me like a bullet train.

I don't want to have one-off sex. I want Mr Johnson to be my partner. My mate.

It's funny. Twenty-hour hours ago I had no idea he was half-bear. Now, I know, deep in my heart and soul that I want to be his.

But, of course, he doesn't want me as *his* mate. He's gonna find someone more mature. A lady bear his own age. That makes sense, even if it hurts like hell.

"It's okay," I say. "If you want to make an exception. I won't regret losing my virginity to you. I mean—" I wave a hand. "I've been fantasizing about it for so long."

He sighs. "That wasn't what I meant, Blair."

I frown. "I don't understand?"

"I mean, I'm only going to mate you if it's *forever*. If I give you my mark and we mate for life."

My heart beats fast. "A-are you saying you want to be with me, like, long-term?"

He nods. "You're the one for me, Blair. All these years I've watched over you, seeing you grow up into this incredible woman. There's never been anyone else in my heart."

I blink. "You've watched over me?"

He nods. "Yup. Over the years, I've stayed close, making sure nobody hurt that beautiful soul of yours. I followed you to Oakdale. I just wanted you to have a happy life, after all you've been through."

"You did all that for me?"

"It's the least I'd do." He takes my hands and holds them gently.

"That's how you were there, the second my ex-boss went psycho?"

"Yup. I knew it was coming. Guess I should've intervened earlier, but I wanted to stay out of sight."

I take a deep breath, the news running through my veins like honey.

"I love you, Blair, you know that?"

My breath catches, and I see the truth of his words glowing in his eyes. They're no longer ice blue, but dark and stormy. "Oh, I've loved you for a long time, Mr Johnson," I manage to say. "I want to be yours."

With a growl, he sweeps me off my feet. "Then I'm gonna claim you, Blair."

He strides down the hallway with me in his arms. I feel so protected. Desired. My whole body is throbbing with the knowledge that just below me is Mr Johnson's huge, erect cock, dying to get to me.

8

Zachary

If I pinch myself, I'm sure I'll wake up. Because there's no way that Blair Callahan is naked in my arms, looking up at me with lust in her eyes, her pussy dripping wet because she wants me so bad.

Everything's happened so fast, and a part of my brain is still screaming, *this ain't right. You don't deserve someone as pure and beautiful as Blair.* But I know, deep in my soul that she's the one. The one I'm supposed to be with.

She was once a kid I was looking out for; now she's the woman I'm supposed to spend the rest of my life with.

My cock is pulsating like a heat-seeking missile, leading us both to the bedroom, and I have to fight the urge to hurtle in there like a wild beast. My bear is scrabbling under my skin, desperate to give Blair its mark before she changes her mind.

That's not how these things work, buddy, I tell it.

Before I even think of forcing my cock into her tight little pussy, I'm gonna make sure she's all but begging for it. That's the only way I can make this right with my conscience.

I kick open the door and lay her down on the bed. The white comforter is a perfect backdrop to her lovely young body. She lies on her back, legs together. I let my gaze sweep over her, from her full, cherry-red lips, to her pert little tits, to her little pink slit.

I can look, because she's mine now. I don't have to be ashamed of my desire anymore.

But when I raise my gaze to those huge golden eyes of hers, I get a jolt in my chest, because she's suddenly looking a little shy.

"There's no rush," I tell her. "We can take it real slow. Nothing's gonna happen that you're not ready for."

She breaks into a smile, and stares at my cock. "Oh, I'm ready. I've been waiting for this for a long, long time. I'm just kind of embarrassed because I've never done anything before."

She's precious. Too darn precious.

"You said you'd been fantasizing about doing this with me?"

Her cheeks turn a beautiful shade of pink. "Maybe."

"You were thinking about it when you were touching yourself yesterday?"

She gets a naughty look. "Were you watching me for long?"

I grunt out a laugh. "Long enough, young lady. Touching yourself in my bed…" I shake my head.

"It was bad, wasn't it?"

A fresh charge of desire burns through me. She's enjoying this.

"You wanna be my bad girl?"

She nods eagerly.

"Show me then. Show me how you were touching yourself."

She hesitates, then slowly, she slides her slender hand down to her pussy.

I watch, mesmerized, as she rubs it back and forth, spreading her wetness around. Then she opens her legs a little.

"Oh, you're a bad girl," I growl, as I get a good look at her little pussy for the first time. It's so pink and perfect. All tight and neat and untouched. Then she spreads herself with two fingers and gets to work on her little clit.

Her finger circles fast and her forehead creases in concentration, but soon she stops and gives me a burning look. "I like it better when you do it," she says.

She doesn't need to ask me twice.

And as soon as I touch her, she cries out.

"Gosh, I love the way you make me feel, Mr Johnson," she says.

I let off another growl. I'm all out of telling her to call me Zach. If this is her thing, so be it.

All I know is I've gotta be inside her. I slide a finger

in. She's so wet, but so tight. Only room for a single finger at most. She shudders and jerks as I slide in and out of her, getting her ready for the assault of my cock. She's real sensitive, my girl.

"What were you thinking about yesterday?" I demand.

"I was imagining what your…." She nods at my dick. "Your… Johnson was like."

I can't resist a grin as I take my aching dick in my hand. It feels about ready to burst. All heavy and swollen. I've got doubts that it's gonna fit inside her. I'll have to go real slow.

"Does the reality match up?"

She bites her lip. "It's real big."

"Well, you'd better get used to it, because it's the only one you're ever gonna have."

She blinks. "What if I can't—?"

"Oh, you will. Because you're my mate." My beast drives me on and before I know it, I'm crouching between her thighs, running my hand up and down my aching shaft.

Shit. Too much; too fast.

"What happened in your fantasy?" I ask.

"Well, you were watching me through the window—"

"Just like in reality."

"Uh huh." She giggles. "And you got so turned on, you took out your cock and started jerking off."

"Mm… hmm." Fuck, she's starting to spasm around my finger. I need to get her close to the brink. It's the only way I'm gonna fit this monster inside her. "And then?"

"Then you couldn't control yourself, and you burst into the cabin, shoved the door open, and just *took me.*"

With a roar of need, I slip my finger out of her and replace it with the tip of my cock. Her eyes flutter closed and she spreads her thighs wider.

Fuck, what a sight.

When I slide my dick up and down between her lips, her sweet mouth falls open and she starts to pant.

"You on anything, baby?" I ask.

She frowns. "No."

"You know there's a chance…?"

"Oh, yes."

My chest glows as I gaze down at her in wonder. She's all spread out, fertile, ready for everything I've got to give her.

I take a deep breath and start to enter my girl's tiny pussy for the first time.

9

Blair

*F*uck. It's really happening. This moment I've fantasized about for years. Never thought in my wildest dreams that it would happen. But here it is. My vision is blurry, I'm turned on like crazy, and Mr Johnson… Mr Johnson is arching over me, all wild and fierce-looking. His huge, thick cock is between my thighs. Forcing its way into me. It's hot and I can feel it pulsing with his desire.

It's not gonna fit… it's not gonna fit…

Damn. It's going into me. His big, thick johnson is opening me up. I feel my muscles spreading for him, and…*ahh!* That hurts.

"Easy…" He pulls out again. "No rush." He's looking down into my face, such love and concern etched into his handsome features, it makes it all better.

"Take it. Take it rough," I tell him. "I want to remember it like this."

Something shifts in his expression, and he looks kinda feral. I shiver, sensing his beast close to the surface.

"You sure about this, baby?"

"Uh huh. Very."

A growl escapes his lips, and he plunges his cock in again.

Fuck! There's a sharp, tearing sensation and stars explode behind my eyelids. "Are you inside me?" I gasp out.

"Almost." He gives one more thrust and hits home.

My pussy is throbbing. His thick cock is buried inside me. Mr Johnson has got my virginity.

"Wow," I mutter. "That's… that's a lot."

A slow smile tugs at his lips. "I've got your sweet cherry, honey."

He lifts my legs up over his shoulders, so I'm bent almost in half, and he starts to thrust.

"*Ahh!*" I cry out again. "Too much… Wait… *Ohh…* okay, that feels good." I giggle. "Don't stop."

So, this is sex, this awesome friction, where every little movement feels *unbelievable*. And the feeling is building and building.

"You gonna come for me, sweetheart?" he grits out. Mr Johnson has never looked as sexy as he does now. Wild, passionate. His huge pecs and biceps rippling with every thrust. "Come around my johnson," he says.

That does it.

My pussy spasms out of control, and I explode, all

around Mr Johnson's cock. I cling to him tight, riding this beautiful train. He keeps on thrusting while I climax, drawing out my orgasm. My pussy is gripping him like it never wants to let him go.

"So goddamn beautiful," he growls. "What did I do to deserve you?"

When I'm done; all weak and exhausted, he turns me in his arms, moving me exactly how he wants me. He's got me on my side, one leg pointing toward the ceiling. He's rough, passionate and I love it.

Finally, I'm on my front, up on my hands and knees.

He plunges into me, hands gripping my ass. "Blair," he growls. "You're mine now."

I feel something sharp and hot on the back of my neck. He's got the nape of my neck between his teeth, like he's holding me still while he plows into me.

Rough, hard, animalistic thrusts. His hips hammer me as he goes faster and faster. And I'm coming again, throbbing around his huge girth.

Then he lets off a roar that's pure bear. A moment later, something hot and relentless floods my womb. His seed.

I'm still shuddering as he pulls me down into his arms and holds me tight against his big, strong familiar body. *I'm his now.* The thought runs through me like warm honey. *I'm his mate.*

10

Zach

I woke up a couple of times during the night, my bear insisting on checking on my mate. Each time, Blair was nestled into my arms, snoring gently. But now, when I awake for the day, she's all sprawled out. Face buried in the pillow, long maple-syrup colored hair fanning out around her. The comforter has drifted down and her lovely back is bare. Real carefully, so I don't wake her, I move her hair off her shoulder, and the sight that greets me sends an electric current through my whole body.

My mark.

I always wondered how it would look on my mate's back. I never gave it to Kayla's mom. Somehow, I knew she wasn't the one. She was always asking me for it, but I kept putting her off. I always suspected she was interested in other guys, and then she left. So I guess I was right.

But with Blair, I didn't have a choice. There was no way my beast was gonna leave her unmarked. As soon as I buried my cock in her virgin pussy, it was getting ready to sink its canines into her soft neck. To give her the mark that bonds us together, forever. That means she's mine to love and protect, always.

I'll never regret that. She's my girl; I know it. My beast knows it. For the first time in my adult life, it's calm. It's quit its relentless pacing and fretting, and finally let me rest. This is the best night's sleep I've had in years. Thanks to this little angel.

As I lift the comforter up to cover her shoulders, guilt flickers in my chest. She's so tiny, so delicate. I didn't mean to be so rough with her last night. I was planning to take it real slow, kiss her from head to toe. Worship every perfect part of her.

Then my bear took over. Guess I can't blame it. It's been waiting a long, long time for this.

But she seemed to like it like that. The way she kept coming and coming... all wild and uninhibited. *Take it rough,* she told me.

A smile tugs at my lips, and right on cue, my cock turns hard as a rock.

She really said that.

My little, tough girl. Like she's always been. But now she's a mature woman who wants my cock inside her.

The thought makes my head feel too full.

Things like this don't happen to a guy like me. I've gotten so used to being alone, to losing people, it felt like that was life's plan for me. But turns out Blair was the plan. My fated mate.

She stirs and gives a sleepy moan. Is she waking up?

Nope, she's just turning onto her side. I hold still, taking in the delicate curve of her spine, her perfect, velvety skin. Then I get up to make coffee.

Unbelievably, the snow is still coming down. I can hardly see out of the kitchen window, and outside, it's piled up more than waist deep. They say it's the biggest blizzard in over a decade. And here I am, snowed in with my girl.

I can't help whistling a little tune as I fill up two mugs with filter coffee. Two spoons of sugar and extra cream—just how she took it in the diner. Then I carry them into the bedroom.

She's sitting up in bed, the covers wrapped around her. Her eyes turn huge at the sight of me.

I freeze. Has she realized it was all a big mistake?

Then she gets a mischievous quirk to her lips. "Good morning, Mr Johnson," she says.

I remember that I'm buck naked, of course, and my cock is hard because I've been thinking about her, as usual.

I set the coffees down on the nightstand and sit on the side of the bed. "Blair, you're my mate now. You definitely can't call me Mr Johnson anymore."

"Even though I've had your johnson inside me?" Her gaze drops deliberately to my cock.

Under her attention, it turns even harder. "Especially because you've had my johnson inside you."

"Awww." She pretends to pout.

I gather her up in my arms and kiss her. She's extra gorgeous like this, soft from sleep, with her hair all mussed.

She sighs, clinging to me, like she can't get enough of my rough ol' body.

My bear pushes at my skin, desperate to claim her again, but I shove it back down. I'm gonna tend to her little pussy first, make sure that beast of mine didn't do her an injury.

"Think I'm about ready to have it inside me again," she murmurs against my lips, and she reaches out and closes her hand around my cock. It surges in her hand.

Holy hell.

"I'm just gonna check first," I tell her.

"Check what—?" She squeaks in surprise as I flip her onto her back and spread her thighs.

She's so wet already. I haven't even touched her yet and her lips are glistening with her pussy juices.

She squirms a little as I spread her lips with my fingers.

"Did I hurt you?"

"Uhh... no.. it's just..." She covers her face with her hands. She feels shy like this. It's delightful. And the more I spread her, the wetter she gets. I stare at her pussy in wonder. What a perfect little thing. Pink and perfectly proportioned. Her clit is a little pink pearl, and her labia are like rose petals. But her entrance looks a little red and torn.

"Looks a little sore where I broke through your hymen," I tell her.

"Ohh," she murmurs.

"But don't worry, I'm gonna kiss it better," I growl. Then I dip my head and taste her pussy for the first time.

It's so soft and sweet. Caramel and cotton candy, mixed together. My bear purrs in delight.

When I run my tongue the length of her slit, she shudders.

At first, I tease her, flicking my tongue everywhere but her clit. Before long, she starts jerking her hips around and tugging on my hair. "Need it here," she mutters.

When I finally drag my tongue over her clit, she almost levitates. Her hips make little jerks, and she grinds on my face. So darn sexy. I keep going, licking that sweet little slit with everything I've got.

Soon she starts to tremble. She yanks on my hair, hard. Then, with a wild scream, she comes, right in my face, her honeyed juices gushing out of her.

"Fuck," she mutters. "I love your tongue, Mr Johnson."

"I'm not finished yet," I tell her, and I dive right back in.

She comes two more times, each stronger than the last, then she shuffles away from me and reaches for my cock.

"I want it in my mouth," she says.

Holy crap. "Blair, you don't have to—"

Too late, already, she's on her hands and knees in front of me, and the tip of my dick is disappearing between her sweet cherry lips.

My eyes almost roll back in my head.

The inside of her mouth is silky soft, and the touch of her tongue... it's like velvet, swirling around my swollen head. Before I know it, I'm pushing deeper into her mouth.

But she doesn't freak out. She adjusts her position, and takes it all. I start to thrust in and out. It's too rough. I shouldn't be doing this, I tell myself. But she's acting like she likes it. She opens wide for me, taking me right in the back of her throat. My balls are aching, tight, ready for a release. I can feel the climax welling up in me—

Suddenly, she pulls her mouth off me. "Now I'm ready for your johnson," she says. There's a wicked gleam in her eyes as she lies back and spreads her thighs wide.

I don't hesitate. I press the wet head of my dick up against her opening. And it slides right in.

It's a lot easier this time. She doesn't tense up or whimper in pain. Instead, her pussy grips me tight, like it's trying to draw me in. I push into her in one long thrust.

When I hit home, she gives a wild cry and wraps her legs around me. "So big, but it fits me," she says in a tone of wonder.

"That's because it was made for you," I growl. "Your pussy was made to only stretch out for my cock. It's the only one you'll ever know." I pull out halfway, then I give a big thrust. "It's gonna fuck you day in, day out. So I hope you're ready for that."

"Oh, I am," she gasps out.

I hold myself up on my arms, watching the emotions

drift across her beautiful face as I fuck one orgasm after another out of her.

She's insatiable, my girl. I was worried she wouldn't be able to stand my appetite, but she matches me. The perfect mate for a horny bear shifter. And she comes again and again, her little pussy muscles squeezing my dick, like she's trying to charm my seed out of me.

I'm gonna breed this ripe, fertile little body, I think as I flood her little pussy for the second time. Hope she's ready to bear my cubs.

Blair

The blizzard continues for three more days. How can there be so much snow up in the sky?

"We're real snowed in," Mr Johnson says cheerfully, peering out of the front window. The drift comes up to the window now. I open the door experimentally, and a wall of white greets me, as high as my armpits.

"I wish we could stay like this forever," I say, snuggling in his arms on the couch. The fire is burning in the grate, we're sipping mugs of hot chocolate, and I feel so cozy and loved-up, I could burst.

"We can," Mr Johnson says in a tone of surprise.

I blink. "Don't you have somewhere you need to be?"

He sighs contentedly. "Nope. I pick my own hours. I

don't need a whole lot of material things these days. You have someplace you need to be?"

I shrug. "Nope." And for the first time in my life, that's a good feeling. I used to feel like no one was looking out for me. There was no one to care if I was late for dinner, or absent from family gatherings.

But I was wrong. All that time, Mr Johnson was keeping watch over me, like a big, rugged guardian angel. And now he's right here, in my bed and in my heart.

"I mean, I want to get a job, and all."

He shrugs. "If that's important to you, once the snow melts, we can go into town and find you one."

"Once the snow melts? That could take all winter."

"I know," he says happily. "And in the meantime, I'll have you all to myself."

"You won't get bored of, you know, just hanging out with me?"

"Are you kidding? That's... that's the best thing ever."

My heart gives a little jump. He loves just *being* with me.

"That sounds wonderful, Zach," I say.

A flicker of surprise passes across the features I love. "Zach," he says in an undertone.

"No more Mr Johnson." I raise my head and look into his eyes. I can't believe I used to think they were cold. Now, they're always soft with love.

His chest rises and falls in a massive sigh.

"That makes me real happy, Blair."

"I'm still gonna call your johnson johnson, though," I say.

His lips curl up into a smile. "Guess I'd be kinda disappointed if you didn't."

I SPEND a whole lot of time with his johnson inside me. He's insatiable. He says he's making up for lost time, and so am I. It's my johnson. Only for me. All of him is for me. I can hardly believe it. Still think I'll pinch myself and wake up on the couch in Oakdale and discover this has all been a beautiful dream.

"WHAT IS IT?" I say.

Zach and I are in bed, as usual, buried under his cozy comforter. He's been planting butterfly kisses all over my face, but suddenly he goes still, his sweet breath warming my cheek.

"Someone's driving down here."

I listen hard, hear nothing. "That's not possible?"

"It shouldn't be. But—"

With a groan of regret, he slides out of bed. "Stay here, I'll be back."

Regret sweeps over me, too, as I watch him hauling clothes over his sexy body. "Come back soon," I call.

I try to tune my ears in, just like a shifter. The snow stopped a day ago and it's virtually silent now, the only sounds the chirps of birds and occasional thumps as snow slides off the roof. I hear Zach stride across the cabin, then the front door opens and bangs again. He's going outside.

And I want to know what's going on. I slither out of bed and open the closet. Zach already cleared out a bunch of shelves for me. I pull on jeans, T-shirt, a sweater and socks and follow after him.

Bright sunlight fills the cabin. Somehow, the blizzard has been followed by unusually sunny weather, and the snow is already starting to melt. I open the front door and squint as light reflects off the pure white snow, dazzling me. The air feels fresh and crisp. I can see the marks Zach made in the snow as he walked along the pathway and turned toward his truck. They're not just footprints; each tread looks to be a couple of feet deep.

For a long, long time, the snowy scene is perfectly still. Then there's a crunch of boots, and I can just make out Zach's broad-shouldered figure coming back toward the cabin. My heart leaps.

But he's not alone. There's a much smaller figure behind him. Female? It's wearing a hooded black coat, so it's hard to tell.

Something stirs in me, something hot and possessive.

If I was wearing boots, I'd run out right now, but instead, I wait, tingling with apprehension.

When Zach catches sight of me, he breaks into a smile. But there's something new in his eyes. Something complicated.

And then the figure lifts her head.

"Kayla?" I gasp.

Stockinged feet be damned, I run to her through the thick snow.

So much pain, so much loss and guilt. It doesn't matter. I throw my arms around my best friend and hug her tight.

"Oh god, you're here," she breathes. "I never thought…"

"Let's go inside," Zach said, a laugh in his voice.

We go into the cabin, Kayla peels off her coat and we all stare at each other, looking back through the years.

She still has her old vitality, but she looks different now, more put together. Her home-made piercings are gone, and her hair is no longer fire-engine red, but a subtle shade of copper, expensively styled and high-lighted.

"You're back," Zach says. "I just can't believe it."

A flicker of shame passes across her face and she takes a deep breath. "I'm sorry I haven't kept in contact. But I've dealt with…everything. It felt like the right time to come back."

"You look so good, Kayla," I tell her.

"I second that," Zach says.

"So do you guys—" Kayla looks from her father, to me and back again. Then her smile drops. "Wait a minute—"

Her nose wrinkles, and she takes a deep sniff. "You're together! What the fuck?"

I wince at the gathering rage in her voice.

"Now, Kayla—" Zach's voice is also loud, reminding me of how he used to be when we were teens.

She rounds on me. "I always knew you were after my dad. I could see it in your eyes." She comes up close. Her own eyes spark pure emerald fire.

"I-it wasn't like that," I stammer. "I was just a kid. I didn't understand my feelings."

"Like hell you didn't." She grabs me by the shoulders.

I try to push her away, but she's ten times stronger than me. I see the wildness in her eyes. It was developing when we were teens, but now she's full grown, it's awesome. Terrifying.

She curls her lip, and I see how long and sharp her canines are. "My own father. How long have you been...?" She trails off in disgust.

"Just a few days. Things happened real fast."

"Fast? Like this hasn't been going on for years?" she snarls.

Zach steps behind Kayla, wraps his arms around her and pulls her off me. "I've been looking out for Blair, that was all. Because she had no one. But things developed. We didn't choose it; it was fate."

Despite all the tension, when my eyes meet his, my heart gives a little jump.

But Kayla is struggling in his grasp. I see teeth and claws and suddenly, even he can't hold onto her anymore. Her clothes start to burst apart, and... Kayla is gone and in her place is a big cat. A huge, magnificent jaguar. She tips her head back and roars. It's like a sonic boom, knocking me senseless. She's going to kill me. Rip me right open with her claws. I cower in terror.

Zach tears the front door open again. "Kayla, get out of here!" he bellows, his volume matching her own.

She throws me one last, disgusted look, then she spins, swiping me with her long tail. And she's off, out through the door.

And Zach is tearing his own clothes off. In a flash, his bear bursts out of him, massive and bristling. And he's after her, barreling out into the snow.

A bear and a big cat, charging through the snow. It's an arresting sight. But panic is surging through my veins. She hates me. All the anger, the betrayal in her eyes curls me up inside. She'll never forgive me for this. And maybe Zach won't want to be with my anymore, now that he's seen her again.

I watch until they disappear into the trees, the pain in my heart leaving me breathless. Then I go inside, grab a fresh set of my clothes and lay them out on the doorstep, along with the clothes Zach just took off.

THEY DON'T COME BACK any time soon. What the hell are they doing out there? I pace up and down the cabin. Then to distract myself, I make a fire in the living room.

The daylight fades and shadow falls across the front of the cabin. I sit in the dim light, waiting.

A big crashing sound comes from outside. Then some kind of scuffle.

The front door bursts open.

There they both are, tucking their shirts into their pants. I search their faces anxiously.

"I'm sorry, Blair." Kayla's head is down, like she can't bring herself to look at me. But Zach throws me a small smile, and I feel it—that buzz of connection in my chest. While he was gone, it was an overwhelming ache, a physical pain. But now it's warm, soothing.

"Come here," he says, crooking his finger toward Kayla. "Both of you." Zach motions for me to go first, and we all head into Kayla's old room.

She lets out a gasp. "Oh, my god. All my stuff. You kept it."

"I moved a lot of it from the old house, of course. But I wanted it all to be here in case you ever came back."

She wanders around the room, picking up various things, rubbing them against her cheek or sniffing them. She runs her fingers along the long claw marks gouged into the wall, with a rueful laugh. "I was a nightmare, wasn't I?"

I shrug. "You could be challenging."

"But you never forgot me?"

"I missed you so much, Kayla," I murmur. "I never stopped wondering where you were."

When she finally turns to face us, her eyes are glistening with tears.

"You're not my bio dad, are you?"

Zach hangs his head. "I made a promise—to myself —never to tell. I always loved you as my daughter though, Kayla. And I tried my best with you."

"I know you did," she says, in a whisper. "But I was unmanageable. Feral."

"A handful." He gives a dry laugh.

"I'm so sorry I left you both." Now tears spill down her cheeks. "My animal was out of control. I was worried it'd wind up hurting somebody."

"And now?" Zach asks.

Kayla breaks into a grin. The first unguarded smile since she's been here. "I've met my mate. A tiger."

"I thought so," Zach says, and his eyes shine with pride.

She closes her eyes for a beat. "And I'm happy you two got together. It's gonna take a bit of getting used to. But I can see you belong together. That you're good for each other." She holds out her arms and I run into them.

* * *

IT'S FULLY DARK NOW, and Zach insists on cooking dinner for us all. He refuses my offer of help, and sends me off with Kayla to her room. We sit on her bed and catch up on the years. We laugh and cry non-stop.

"I found my mom," she tells me, knees drawn up to her chest.

"Oh my god. How did it go?"

She swallows hard. "She was scary. Beautiful, but real cold. She said leaving me and dad was the best thing—maybe the only good thing—she ever did. She knew we were two real good people, and she was just gonna screw up our lives. She said Zach did a great job of raising me."

At last, Kayla lifts her head and meets my eyes. "I know you're supposed to be together. I think I knew it even as I was freaking out back there. You're just right for each other. Any fool could see that."

"Thanks, Kayla, that means a lot," I reply, my heart lifting.

· · ·

WE SPEND a long time at the dinner table, eating and catching up, then Kayla stays the night in her old room.

The next morning, she leaves, promising to bring her mate the next time she comes.

Zach and I watch her negotiate the snowy road in her truck. Then we return to the cabin. Our cabin. And fall into each other's arms.

I feel his chest rise and fall. "Thank goodness," I say.

He strokes my hair with his big hand. "That was the missing piece, the only thing I was worried about."

I tilt my head back. There's something different in his eyes. A brand-new peace. His soul is lighter, too. I feel it in my own—that charge of electricity connecting the two of us.

I stroke his beard with my fingertips. "Everything's perfect now," I murmur.

"It sure is," he says happily. Then he sweeps me right off my feet and carries me along the passageway. Back to finish what we started.

EPILOGUE

Three months later

"Will you still be attracted to me when my belly's all big and swollen?" I say. We're lying in bed in the cabin, and Zach is snuggling me in his massive arms, nuzzling my neck with morning kisses.

"More than ever." He runs his big hand over my stomach. "It'll be so sexy."

Tingles of delight run through me. I can't believe how much he wants me. He takes me at least three times every day, and the desire in his eyes only gets stronger. Under his gaze I feel like the most beautiful woman in the world.

"What about when my boobs get really big?"

"Uh huh." He cups them, chafing my nipples in that

way he knows drives me wild. "I can't wait until they're full of milk."

I bite back a moan. "How about when my pussy shuts down?"

He stills for a beat, uncertainty flickering in his eyes. "That part doesn't happen."

I giggle. "It might. When she gets bigger, there won't be space for your johnson."

"Is that right?" He flips around, and suddenly, my legs are spread, and his stubble is grazing my thighs. "There's not a whole lot of space anyway."

"There's just enough—" I sigh as he plants kisses on the sensitive skin of my inner thighs. He's so big, but somehow my pussy manages to accommodate him. Because it was made for him, as he likes to tell me.

"Or, if you're worried, I could just go down on you until the baby comes." He dips his head and lashes my clit with his tongue.

"Ohhh—" I moan. "Remind me what that's like?"

With a growl, he dives right in. His skillful tongue rides my arousal, driving me to the brink. It's not long before I'm clutching at his hair, and crying out his name as I *explode*. Sunlight is coming through the curtains, but all I can see is stars.

"Nope," I say, a minute later.

Zach raises himself up and gives me a questioning look.

I take him in, his huge, hard cock jutting out between his muscular thighs, and a grin spreads across my face. "I still need your johnson."

A feral sound escapes his lips and in another second,

he's on me, eyes blazing with lust. He holds me down as he impales me with his thick cock. Just how I like it. My sexy older mate, possessing me again.

* * *

LATER THAT DAY, I give Zach a curious look as we pull up in front of a grand house on the edge of the forest. It's like a super-sized log cabin. A lodge, I guess you could call it.

"So?" I crook an eyebrow. "What are we doing here?"

He shrugs, then says, all casual, "Thought you might want to live here."

My mouth falls open. "This place is for sale?"

"Yup." He jumps out of the truck and runs around to open the door for me. Then he takes my hand and holds it tight. "Let's go take a look."

It's a beautiful house. Rustic on the outside, but super-cozy inside, with tons of space. There are two stories, a huge basement and a loft.

"Think five bedrooms will be enough?" Zach asks, as I look out of an upstairs window at the endless pines surrounding us. They don't seem sinister anymore. They feel like old friends. He hugs me from behind, gently stroking my belly.

"Oh, I hope so, because this feels like my dream house," I say.

"We can always build an annex at the back if we need to accommodate a few more," he mutters into my hair.

My heart gives a little jump. We both want to have a

big family. At least six, Zach says, which sounds about perfect to me. Our own little bear clan. The big rowdy family I've always dreamed of.

Outside, there's a huge wraparound porch, and beyond that is a wild yard.

"It's just lovely," I breathe.

"We'll get some big rockers. Then you can sit right there, watching me chop wood."

I laugh. It's a long-running joke of ours. Turns out on that first morning, when I woke up and saw him chopping wood outside the cabin, he knew I was watching him. He says he smelled my arousal as soon as he came into the cabin, and he knew he was a goner.

"So?" Zach turns to me as we stroll down the front steps.

"So?" I turn my head to meet his gaze.

"Shall we take it?"

"Can we?"

He laughs. "Baby, you want it, it's yours."

I give a little gasp. I'm not used to things—well, life —happening like this. "Will we have to sell the cabin though?"

"Not a chance." He shakes his head, smiling. "That little place has way too much history. Besides, it might be a good place for our teens to let off steam when they get to be too much."

"Then yes, please. Let's take it!" I hug him tight, my heart rising up high, dreaming of our beautiful future together.

EPILOGUE

Five years later

"That's weird," I say as Zach pulls up in front of our house.

"No kids, huh?"

"Yeah…" I look around as I grab some groceries off the backseat, and we head up the driveway. Our three cubs are *always* outside, no matter the weather. Typical little bear cubs, Zach says.

I look for them in the treehouse and in the little adventure playground that Zach has built in a corner of the yard, but it's all deserted.

"House looks dark, too."

I follow his gaze. There's a little orange glow showing at each window, but no more. "Very strange."

We raise an eyebrow at each other.

When Zach swings open our big wooden front door,

the house is as cozy as ever, but silence greets us. And the hallway is dark. But when I go to flick on the light switch, I hear something—a little squeak of rubber soles on tile, perhaps. Zach touches my shoulder, and puts a finger to his lips.

I drop my hand from the light switch and we keep walking into the house.

"Where are the kids?" I say loudly.

"Maybe they're taking a nap," he replies.

Suddenly, there's an eerie wail, and two white shapes hurtle out of the darkness and wrap themselves around me. I let out a scream.

A moment later, Zach yells and collapses on the ground as a tiny skeleton jumps on his chest. "Arghh! We're being attacked!" he hollers.

"Jessie, Riley, come save us!" I wail.

Three little monsters explode into hilarity.

"*I'm* Jessie!" says the little white sheet that's now staring up at me. Through two little round eyeholes, I can make out my daughter's earnest blue eyes.

I frown. "You're not Jessie. You're a little ghostie. What have you done with my daughter?"

"She's here!" Jessie tears the sheet off her head, cackling uproariously.

"But who's this?" I turn to the other ghostie in mock confusion.

"Liam!" he yells, tearing off his own sheet.

"Thank goodness! I thought you'd been kidnapped."

The kitchen light flicks on. Kayla and her mate, Enzo, are standing behind the island, grinning broadly.

"Surprise!" she says.

"They've been planning that all afternoon," Enzo says, as the kids tear off, chasing each other, accompanied by blood-curdling screams.

"And you've been baking." My mouth waters at the sight of a huge pumpkin pie cooling on a rack.

"Thought we should get in the spirit of things." Kayla takes out a knife and cuts four slices. "They've been asking if they can go trick-or-treating tonight."

"Oh, yeah!" Zach jumps in before I have time to reply.

I shoot him a look of surprise.

"I've always loved Halloween." He rubs his hands together. "I'll take them around Twin Falls this evening."

Kayla smiles at me with a glow of pride. Zach is such an amazing father to Jessie, Riley and Liam. He's so energetic and involved in everything. And Kayla loves him for it. She says he was a great father to her as well. At the time, she thought he was this huge disciplinarian, but now she recognizes that if he hadn't been like that, she would've gotten into real trouble. And he took care of her all those years, even though she wasn't his own.

"I'll come with you?" Enzo offers.

"That'd be great," Zach says happily, clapping him on the shoulder.

The pumpkin pie is delicious. Still warm and perfectly spiced. It reminds me just how much I love this time of year, when the nights are drawing in, and everything turns orange and gold. And it's so much more fun when we're celebrating with our kids.

Kayla puts down her fork and narrows her eyes at

me. "So, you gonna tell us where you've been all afternoon?"

I copy her expression. "If you tell me where you went this morning?"

Her hand drifts down to her belly and she breaks into a grin. "We have some great news."

I let out a scream. "Oh, my god!"

"It's a boy, and he's coming in about six months' time."

I rush over and wrap my arms around her, tears springing to my eyes. Kayla and Enzo have been trying for a baby for a year. It hasn't been easy because they're different species. But it's finally happening. "And everything's going well, right?"

"Yup. He's healthy, and real big." She draws away from me, holding me at arms' length. "And you're pregnant again, right?"

"Yup," I say with a flicker of guilt. Zach and I are so fertile it's embarrassing. He got me pregnant when he took my virginity—just like he warned me he would. Then, eighteen months after Jessie was born, I had Ryan. Then just over a year after that, I had Liam. I *was* planning to wait another year before we tried for number four, but there was that night on our summer vacation when Zach's mom was looking after the kids and… well.

Note to self: if you don't want to get pregnant, don't go for a midnight skinny dip with your gorgeous mate when you're in heat.

"We're eight weeks in," I tell Kayla.

She gasps. "Us, too! Oh my god, I hope we give birth at the same time. That would be awesome."

I give her another big hug. I'm real excited that we'll have babies at the same time, and I'm so glad she feels the same way. We're an unconventional family, but between us we've got enough love for a whole tribe of cubs.

THE END

READ THE OTHER BOOKS IN THE SERIES

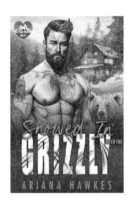

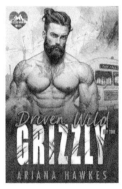

If you like fated-mate romances, with plenty of V-card fun and tons of feels, check out the other books in the series at:

arianahawkes.com/obsessed-mountain-mates

READ MY OTHER OBSESSED MATES SERIES

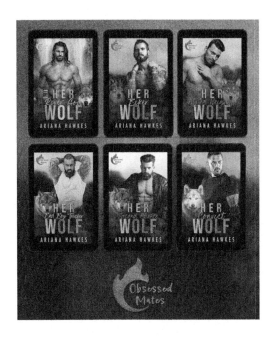

If you like steamy insta-love romance, featuring obsessed, growly heroes who'll do anything for their mates, check out my Obsessed Mates series. All books are standalone and can be read in any order.

Get started at arianahawkes.com/obsessed-mates

READ THE REST OF MY CATALOGUE

MateMatch Outcasts: a matchmaking agency for beasts, and the women tough enough to love them.

★★★★★ "A super **exciting, funny, thrilling, suspenseful and steamy shifter romance series**. The characters jump right off the page!"

★★★★★ "**Absolutely Freaking Fantastic**. I loved every single word of this story. It is so full of **exciting twists that will keep you guessing until the very end** of this book. I can't wait to see what might happen next in this series."

Ragtown is a small former ghost town in the mountains, populated by outcast shifters. It's a secretive place, closed-off to the outside world - until someone sets up a secret mail-order bride service that introduces women looking for their mates.

Get started at arianahawkes.com/matematch-outcasts

MY OTHER MATCHMAKING SERIES

My bestselling *Shiftr: Swipe Left For Love* series features Shiftr, the secret dating app that brings curvy girls and sexy shifters their perfect match! Fifteen books of totally bingeworthy reading — and my readers tell me that Shiftr is their favorite app ever! ;-) Get started at arianahawkes. com/shiftr

★★★★★ "**Shiftr is one of my all-time favorite series**! The stories are funny, sweet, exciting, and scorching hot! And they will **keep you glued to the pages!**"

★★★★★ "**I wish I had access to this app**! Come on, someone download it for me!"

Get started at arianahawkes.com/shiftr

CONNECT WITH ME

If you'd like to be notified about new releases, giveaways and special promotions, you can sign up to my mailing list at arianahawkes.com/mailinglist. You can also follow me on BookBub and Amazon at:

bookbub.com/authors/ariana-hawkes
amazon.com/author/arianahawkes

Thanks again for reading – and for all your support!

Yours,
Ariana

* * *

USA Today bestselling author Ariana Hawkes writes spicy romantic stories with lovable characters, plenty of suspense, and a whole lot of laughs. She told her first story at the age of four, and has been writing ever since, for both work and pleasure. She lives in Massachusetts with her husband and two huskies.

www.arianahawkes.com

GET TWO FREE BOOKS

Join my mailing list and get two free books.

 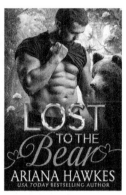

Once Bitten Twice Smitten

A 4.5-star rated, comedy romance featuring one kickass roller derby chick, two scorching-hot Alphas, and the naughty nip that changed their lives forever.

Lost To The Bear

He can't remember who he is. Until he meets the woman he'll never forget.

Get your free books at arianahawkes.com/freebook

READING GUIDE TO ALL OF MY BOOKS

Obsessed Mates

Her River God Wolf

Her Biker Wolf

Her Alpha Neighbor Wolf

Her Bad Boy Trucker Wolf

Her Second Chance Wolf

Her Convict Wolf

Obsessed Mountain Mates

Driven Wild By The Grizzly

Snowed In With The Grizzly

Chosen By The Grizzly

Shifter Dating App Romances

Shiftr: Swipe Left for Love 1: Lauren

Shiftr: Swipe Left for Love 2: Dina

Shiftr: Swipe Left for Love 3: Kristin

Shiftr: Swipe Left for Love 4: Melissa

Shiftr: Swipe Left for Love 5: Andrea

Shiftr: Swipe Left for Love 6: Lori

Shiftr: Swipe Left for Love 7: Adaira

Shiftr: Swipe Left for Love 8: Timo

Shiftr: Swipe Left for Love 9: Jessica

Shifter Holiday Romances

Bear My Holiday Hero

Ultimate Bear Christmas Magic Boxed Set Vol. 1

Ultimate Bear Christmas Magic Boxed Set Vol. 2

Printed in Great Britain
by Amazon